unraveling

unraveling

michelle baldini | **lynn biederman**

poems by gabrielle biederman

delacorte press

Published by Delacorte Press
an imprint of Random House Children's Books
a division of Random House, Inc.
New York

Delacorte Press and colophon are registered trademarks of
Random House, Inc.

Visit us on the Web! www.randomhouse.com/teens

Educators and librarians, for a variety of teaching tools, visit us at
www.randomhouse.com/teachers

Library of Congress Cataloging-in-Publication Data is available on request.
ISBN: 978-0-385-73540-7 (trade) ISBN: 978-0-385-90521-3 (lib. bdg.)

The text of this book is set in 12-point Goudy.

Book design by Kenny Holcomb

Printed in the United States of America

10 9 8 7 6 5 4 3 2 1

First Edition

for our mothers

For my mother,
Judith West Edelman,
who always says
"Even spots can become
stripes." It's hard to say
who held the baton out
first, but I'm so grateful
that we are each holding
on to an end.—L.B.

For my mother, Linda
Cameron, for reflections
of inspiration, for being
herself and for never
giving up.—M.B.

ACKNOWLEDGMENTS

The authors are grateful to the following people:

Stephanie Lane, our superperceptive and endlessly receptive editor at Random House, for finding Amanda's story compelling enough to shape and shepherd it to fruition. From the start, your dedication to this project has been far beyond the call of duty. No amount of thanks is enough.

Ginger Knowlton, our agent, for being diplomatic, accessible and crazy nice, just for starters. Thank you for all your advice, and the times we're asked who our agent is, when we get to toss our heads back and say, "Oh, Ginger Knowlton of Curtis Brown." Excuse us while we fluff our hair.

Lisa Pazer, for her tireless assistance from the original manuscript, through many revisions and permutations, to its final landing. You are an incredible wordsmith and have the best laugh in the world. *Unraveling* would not be what it is without you.

Judith Rovenger, for being *that* professor. *Unraveling* began because of you and your young adult literature classes. Your belief in us, encouragement and niceness are the foundation and karma of this book.

Gaby Biederman, *Unraveling*'s poet, for also being our #1 YA reader and critic extraordinaire.

Lynn also expresses heartfelt thanks to:

My daughter, Gaby. It was *your* conviction about my ability that kept me going. Thank you forever for that, for all the times we obsessed together over a single word or sentence, and for sharing your spirit, soul and delicious quirkiness with me—I hope you always will.

My son, Brad. Thank you for being such a fan, for your unwavering belief that *Unraveling* would be published, and for always asking me about my day. Some people say that teenagers think the world revolves around them. They've never met the likes of you.

My dad, for proudly calling me "auteur, auteur," Auntie M. for coining "Quilly" and my brother, for anointing me "Pencil Neck" since we were kids, and making me laugh, even when my neck was strained from hunching over my keyboard.

My phenomenal friends, for making me feel like a famous author. Bestseller shmestseller—you've all enriched my life more than any blockbuster could; to Robin Scheman, for analyzing everything including my bio-shots as only you could; Martha Frankel, for Celeste on my porch and you on deck—like *Hats & Eyeglasses*, I'll always surface for you; Dave Toy, for fortune cookie work needed yesterday; Karyn Jenkins and Dinah Baken, for design advice at a moment's notice; and Paula Desperito and everyone at Bedford Free Library, for their overwhelming enthusiasm.

Finally, to my husband, Eric, stellar neck and back rubber; sous-chef; primary grocery shopper, procurer and provider of all things needed and desired; steady-Eddie source of reason, balance, friendship and love: Thank you, my honey, for seeing me through this. Look out, though . . . another's on the way.

Michelle would like to express her undying gratitude to the following people:

First, to my husband, Artie Baldini, for holding down the fort in the rain, and for late-night snacks, morning coffee, inexhaustible neck rubs, eleventh-hour errands—and mostly for listening with tired ears. Very tender thanks to my children, Stephanie, Michelle, Matthew and David, for their commitment and devotion to family: Thank you for enduring an absentee mother at times and for helping me realize my dream. I hope you fulfill all of yours—big and small.

To the best in-laws ever, Brigida and Arturo Baldini, who remind me that I am the engine. Special thanks to Anna Morelli—my godsend—for doing everything whenever I needed it. And to Gina Baldini for her endless support and love.

Hugs to my siblings—Carey Young, for sharing stories with a flashlight past bedtime, and Trista Karl and Ronnie Cooper, for believing in their big sister. To Dave Cameron, for your enlightenment—Misfit Land should never exist.

Marion Tomas-Griffin, for keeping me grounded all the way from California; Rose Hoey, for her sound direction early on; and my morning, afternoon and nighttime sounding boards—Julie Trego, Raquel Berroteran and Caroline Mourad.

Carolyn Brodie, one of the most amazing women I know—thank you for your counsel and for possessing the most miraculous gift of revealing the very best in the lives you touch.

Finally, I am forever grateful to Cecily Truett, for making me believe I was a leading star, even when I was the zaniest creature that ever walked this earth—every budding woman should be so blessed as to have you by her side. Thank you for your honest reviews on the original manuscript and for getting Amanda out of the cabin.

We would also like to thank Kenny Holcomb, *Unraveling*'s talented designer; Steve Ross, kind mentor; David Levithan, for his encouragement; and everyone at Delacorte Press.

1

The first Chinese fortune I collected the summer I hooked up with Paul—the guy some might consider my first—read:

> **The smart thing is to prepare for the unexpected.**

I should have taken it more seriously. Fortunes can be like little instructions for life; they may not fit yours at that particular moment, after that particular meal of kung pao chicken, but eventually they will. Trust me on this.

2

My mother, Susan Sturtz Himmelfarb, could best be described as uptight, controlling and ultraorganized, like an efficiency expert, which I think is actually a real job for some people. The Captain, my mother, prides herself on being able to complete tasks faster than anyone. I'm the total opposite—a march-to-the-beat-of-my-own-drum, at-my-own-pace type. The Captain says I'm impulsive and that I don't "do things the way the world does."

She has issues with the length of my "hour" showers, how I pull back my curtains or sleep on top of the duvet cover, put socks on before pants and makeup before shirt, how I tie my laces (still do the two-loop thing), open an envelope, hold a pencil, pour a drink and blow my nose. Even how I spray on my perfume and brush my teeth is apparently "not how any other normal teenager in the universe would." My study habits, friends, grades (except English) and "sarcastic, fresh mouth" are also unacceptable to The Captain. Melody, my sister, is *always* acceptable, unless of course she's whining. At least I was under less scrutiny on vacation. One reason I wanted to get to Myrtle Beach.

But, more important, I couldn't wait to meet up with Paul. To have him hug me and make me forget about all the crap I had to deal with. He spent the entire summer in the oceanfront Grand Strand Condos; we went down to our condo only in August, renting it out the rest of the season. Last August I flirted with Paul whenever I got the chance, combing the beach looking to "coincidentally" walk by him. Then, on our last night, while my parents were out, I bumped into him at my neighbor's party. We talked for a long time. He told me he was seventeen and going into his senior year and that the following summer he would be lifeguarding again. I lied and said I was going to be a sophomore. We kissed and he felt me up over my shirt.

I spent ninth grade IM'ing and texting with Paul, and talking nonstop about him to my best friend, Paige. It got so bad that a few weeks before I was going to see Paul again, Paige joked that she was taking up a collection for me so I could fly there already, and she could finally stop hearing about him.

But we didn't fly the seven hundred miles, we drove.

And the car ride from Larchmont, New York, to Myrtle Beach showed signs of impending doom long before we reached our overnight stop.

It began with my dad popping in his traveling tunes CD and happily singing along in his own world. Dad, La-La Man, could care less that he sang the wrong words and was way off-key. The Captain cared. She ejected his CD after one song because she just couldn't "take the noise any longer." All *I* wanted to do was listen to my iPod and write in my journal, but my prissy, pimple-free little sister, Melody, had to be so annoying with her *I'm so good, I'm so good, I'm so good, good, good* dance, sticking her bony fingers up in the air as she listed, in *perfect* order, every capital of every state starting with Washington and going around the country. When this agony ended, Loser Daughter (me) was forced to "stay focused" and answer trivia-card questions my mother rattled off, instead of zoning out.

Even worse was being trapped in my parents' battlefield. They'd been bickering more than usual, ever since they started planning Melody's bat mitzvah. My dad wanted to cut costs, but my mother was letting Melody choose last-minute extras with the party planner and the *event*, a month away, was turning into one of those huge, overdecorated, ten motivators with the DJ type things. It didn't seem fair that The Captain was making such a big to-do. Mine had been a simple luncheon in the temple social hall.

La-La Man was trying to ignore The Captain's coaching

on the speed limit, which lane to drive in, and how close our car was to the one in front of it. I could tell by the way he was chewing on the inside of his mouth that he couldn't completely tune her out. He was the official driver but The Captain was our official commander in chief.

By the time we screeched into the hotel, my father was in an obviously bad mood. He was gripping the steering wheel so tightly his knuckles were white. The latest dispute was partly my fault, because thirty minutes before we stopped, I broke Rule #501: use proper English when speaking. I caused a fight by saying that I had to "pee" instead of "urinate," which prompted my mother, the ex–English teacher, to lecture me *again* on using appropriate terminology. Dad told her to stop correcting what she called my "vulgar slang," which led to my mother sternly correcting him not to correct her correcting me. This was classic Cap, being *Firm on Terms*.

The check-in process enraged my mother even more. The Captain stood at the front desk, clearing her throat, tapping her fingers on the counter and making a point of checking her watch. Dad, back into La-La mode, padded around the hotel lobby, flipping through activity brochures and getting the lay of the land—unnecessarily, since we were only staying one night. The desk lady was "asleep at the switch." My mother snarled a little too loudly to Melody, "If she moved any more slowly, she'd be operating in reverse." When we finally got the keys, the plan was to drop our bags in the room and bolt to the pool—a rare departure from standard Captain

Procedures requiring us to first unpack our bags, even just overnight ones.

> A criticism a day keeps
> your child away.

In no time at all, my parents and Malady were waiting impatiently for me. They were already changed while I was still digging around for the yellow bikini that highlights my ass. Finally, I made it into the bathroom, pulled off my shorts and noticed it—a spot of dark red in my brand-new Victoria's Secret thong.

It was the sign of my "bitch visiting," as Aunt Jen, Mom's sister, says when she gets her period and comes to our house with bad cramps. She'll whisper to me, "I'm being bitch-slapped," so The Captain, aka Mrs. Proper English Terminology, can't hear.

I stared at my thong. "Shit," I muttered to myself but The Captain's Superwoman antennae picked it up.

"What did you say? Amanda, what are you doing in there for so long?" she demanded.

"Please, go ahead without me." I peeled off my thong and threw it in the corner of the scuzzy floor.

"Pick up the pace. Now. N.O.W. Let's go. I'm not going to spend another vacation with all of us waiting on *you*. How long can it possibly take a person to put on a simple bathing suit?"

Typical question. She was always asking why it took me so long to do something.

"Amanda? *Amanda*. I'm talking to you. You acknowledge me."

She was always complaining that I didn't acknowledge her. Funny how I felt exactly the same way.

Finally I whispered, "I *really* need something. Can you plea—"

"What *now*? Open this door."

I wrapped a towel around myself and unlocked the door. She plowed in, accidentally dropping her sunglasses. "That's just great," she said, very annoyed. She was in her halter-top bathing suit with a wrap neatly tied at the side. Melody looks more like The Captain than I do—blond hair, brown eyes, fair skin and the same mouth. Her frame is more like Dad's, though—tall and lanky. My body resembles my mother's—petite and curvy—but that's it. My features and coloring mirror Dad's. We both have almond-shaped blue eyes and frizzy (the extent of the frizz depends on the weather) strawberry blond hair. My pointy chin, however, came out of nowhere.

When The Captain reached down to pick up her sunglasses, she spotted my bloodstained thong. "Amanda, why didn't you keep track of your cycle on the calendar?" Her question reminded me of that fortune I had tucked in my pocket just hours before, when we'd stopped for lunch—*The smart thing is to prepare for the unexpected.*

"God, Mom. My period's on its own schedule."

"Amanda, we just went over this last month and two

7

months before *that* when I had to drop everything and come get you at school."

"Right, and I told you *then* it's not coming on the exact day it's supposed to. I tried to chart it, *Mom*, but I'm not regular. It's not my fault."

"Amanda, please. I don't have the head for this. Please try not to be your difficult self for once."

Please try not to be yourself, I almost said.

Malady whined from outside the door. "God. Now we're missing the last of the sun for the day. I need the sun to dry up my cold."

"Poor Malady," I yelled, mimicking her whine.

"I've told you not to call her that."

"Shut up, loser!" Malady screamed back.

"Melody, that's enough," The Captain warned. "You two go ahead." I imagined La-La Man and Melody saluting the door, turning on their heels and filing out.

My sister was just what I didn't need—someone who always agreed with The Captain. Twenty-seven months separated Melody and me, but we were light-years apart—total opposites, like my mother and Aunt Jen.

"She's in Mandy Land," La-La Man said to no one in particular as he shut the door.

My mother left the bathroom and came back with a box of tampons. I stared at it. The idea of pulling something foreign out of me I could deal with. It was the sticking something *in* me that, like, freaked me—another reason the idea of losing my virginity really scared me.

8

"I packed pads," I told her, putting a stop sign up to the box she was holding out to me.

"Pads again? Just use a tampon. Amanda, don't make a cause célèbre out of this."

"A what?"

"Don't make this into some big drama," she said, shoving the box into my hand.

"But I'm not ready for those," I said.

"Readiness has nothing to do with it—it's what you do, period. Hurry up! I'll meet you at the pool."

I could've pointed out the pun on *period* to Mrs. Proper English Terminology, but *menses* would be the correct word, and I had more important goals, bigger fish to fry. I needed to get to the pool for the last two hours of decent sun. It was my last chance to bronze up for Paul.

The Captain's impatience with me and the tampon wasn't just about her usual impatience with me, it was also this thing she had about being weak. Lots of things smelled weak to her, like my not wanting to go to school with "only" a 99.9-degree temperature or not trying out for the all-county swim team because I knew Courtney Flakey, the girl I hated more than any other in my entire school, would beat me and win the only spot. And, of course, pads—using one was, for some weird reason, a sign of weakness. Aunt Jen said their mom had called them diapers and told them to use tampons from their first period since they weren't babies, just pains who could *make* babies and cause her worse problems.

My mother said pads hold a woman back and compared the

pad to a crutch, unlike the tampon, which she said gives you freedom to do everything as if you weren't menstruating.

> **Take no prisoners—**
> **adolescence means war.**

Pinching the tiny printed instructions out of the box, she pointed to diagrams illustrating, in four-step bubble pictures, a tampon making its way into the crotch of a squatting woman. Sounding like a cross between *Tampons for Dummies* and Emily Post's *Teen Etiquette*, she left me with the task at hand. Aye-aye, Captain.

I studied the instructions and reluctantly assumed the position.

Ready . . . Aim . . . Fire!

I tried to get the tampon in, I really did. Several times. But I just couldn't do it. It felt like it was the wrong angle or something. It made me wonder what a guy's you-know-what would feel like in me. With every failed attempt, my fear of doing it with Paul grew. He *must* be wider and probably *longer* than a slender tampon. I pictured myself getting split apart like a fortune cookie.

"@#$%! You stupid @#$%ing cardboard piece of @#$%!" I screamed at the tampon. Step three was a total no-go; the missile wouldn't launch!

I was concerned about not following The Cap's orders. But I had no choice. She was in her everything-is-making-me-angry mood, and I didn't want to take too long. So I stuck a pad to my bikini bottom and hurried to the pool.

Immediately I noticed a group of cute guys sitting in a cluster of lounge chairs at the deep end playing cards. One guy elbowed the guy next to him. In my peripheral vision, I saw them scanning me. I'm no beauty queen, but I have some boobage. And to provide a better contour of my bottom—my *derriere extraordinaire*—I retied my sheer wrap tighter around myself. My bubble butt is one of my best features, according to Paige.

My worst feature, my out-of-control frizz bomb, was tamed into a bun, the straggler pieces were pulled away from my face with cool shades and I had done a Picasso-esque job of covering a chin zit. I know it's sick, but I imagined being a stripper—their eyes on me, waiting for me to reveal my treasures. I felt transformed from average human to sun goddess.

> **From beast to beauty we go.**

My dad taught me how to swim by throwing me in the deep end first. This was pretty much how I led my life. The Captain knew this better than anyone. She was always anticipating what I was about to do—her antennae tuned in even for future screwups.

I decided to saunter toward the diving board, walking along the opposite side of the pool from where the guys were sitting. Strutting past The Captain at the shallow end, I caught her crinkled-brow, squinty-eye look. I read it as general annoyance and ignored it, instead of letting her poke a hole in Mandy Land and send me spiraling back down to Earth.

I dropped my wrap and shades to the side of the diving board and climbed up the ladder. At the top, I tossed my head and arched my back. I clasped my hands and stretched my arms out way in front of me, nonchalantly cracking my neck and looking over the pool. No one was in it—the stage was all mine. I dove in. I was a beautiful acrobat soaring through the air in a perfect pike, slicing into crystal-clear water. I was free, cruising, gliding to the bottom. The water brushed gloriously along my body, light, cool and tingly.

That's when I felt it—the water. *There*. I grabbed at my crotch in horror. The pad had escaped. Panicked, I spun around to see *it* floating toward the surface. Like in a slow-motion nightmare, I flailed frantically through the water, trying to reach it before it surfaced. *Reach it or drown*, I was thinking as my chest ached for air. I was able to snatch it, clench it between my fingers and pop my head above the surface just before my lungs exploded. As my eyes adjusted, I casually scanned the perimeter of the pool to scout out who might have been watching. One of the guys was looking at me, but I couldn't be sure he had any clue I was clasping a used pad in my fist.

As I made my way over to the side of the pool, The Captain and Malady sat up. La-La Man pressed his nose into his *Sports Illustrated* magazine. His bristly hair stuck out from the sides of his Go Easy hat. Mortified and ready to vomit, I had only one hope: to discreetly dispose of my pad in the skimmer basket. But then I noticed that the trapdoor was off. This meant the pad, brown and gross and triple in size, would break the surface the second I let go of it.

As if she'd read my thoughts, Malady leaned over the edge of the pool and whispered too loudly, "That's going to clog the filter."

My mother glared at her.

"What?" Malady said, slumping back into her lounge chair.

> The gene pool could use
> a little chlorine.

Ignoring my disease of a sister, I scrunched the pad in my hand and climbed out of the pool as casually as I could. A few magazines were at the end of Malady's chair. I decided to grab one on my way to the garbage can. "Hey. Those are mine," she said, pushing down on them with her feet. I yanked one right out from under her and then quickly rolled it around the dirty, wet pad. I ran to the garbage can against the fence and dumped it in. The magazine (and nasty insert) hit the metal bottom with a thud. I was dripping and freezing, but the pad was finally away from me and the worst was over. Except as I headed back to my family to get a towel, I heard snickering from the group of guys. And just then my mother gasped.

"A-MAN-DA HIM-MEL-FARB! Cover yourself."

Frantically, I looked down and saw a dark red stream trickling down my leg. My mother sprang out of her chair, grabbed a towel and threw it at me. I caught it, wrapped it around me, sopped up my humiliation and hurried away from the pool. I was no sun goddess—just the same old Himmel*fart*.

3

It takes more than good
memory to have good memories.

Shortly after *The Great Pad Escape*, my dad followed me up
to the rooms. He knocked lightly on the adjoining door and
whispered "Amanda." I pretended not to hear. As soon as
the TV went on in his room, I called Paige.

"What's wrong?" she asked the minute she heard my voice.

As soon as I heard hers, I started crying. "I topped
Himmel*fart*."

"Oh no."

In seventh grade I had been dubbed "Himmel*fart*" by
Courtney Flakey, my number-one enemy and rival on the
school swim team. I had farted during this standardized test our
entire class was taking in a silent auditorium. As I ran past her
down the middle aisle, a succession of loud bubble farts following my ass, she sang, "There goes A-man-da Him-mel-fart."

The name got flung at me several times during my otherwise unnoticeable middle school existence, and, because of Fakey Flakey, it graduated and moved with me across campus to the high school.

"Oh yes, I topped it," I wept. I told Paige the story of the biggest, most buoyant bloody pad in the universe. I stopped only to blow my nose or to repeat what I was saying in my pathetic sobbing voice.

"I'm so sorry. I wish I could be there with you right now."

"Me too."

"That really sucks. How embarrassing," she said gently.

"I'm such a dork . . . such a loser. . . ."

"Stop. No, you're not."

"I walked out to the pool thinking I was so hot . . ."

"You are . . . you're so pretty. I wish I had your figure. . . . I'm still an A-cup."

"Shut up. You look good."

"Whatever. What matters is you're never gonna see those guys again."

"Yeah. I guess." I had finally stopped crying. "How about how nice The Cap was to me? I can always count on her and Malady."

"They're so out of control."

"Know what? I hope Malady gets hers right through her bat mitzvah dress."

"Ouch. I forget how mean you can be, Amanda *Sturtz* Himmelfarb. That would be totally cruel for her first time."

"Yeah . . . not as bad as *Cruel at the Pool*."

"You and your fight titles."

We talked until I felt better, and then I promised Paige I would try to forget the whole thing and watch TV or read.

Malady and The Cap stayed at the pool, lingering and then eating dinner there at the bar. Later when they returned from their private time together, Malady said loudly from the other room, "You will not believe how great the burgers are here. Yum." Unlike me, Malady would do *anything* for The Captain's attention. I was busy trying to stay under her radar. I had taken Paige's advice and crawled into bed with *Vanishing Acts* by Jodi Picoult.

My mother called "Manda" halfheartedly. "Are you hungry?"

"No."

"Do you want to talk about what happened?"

"No, I'm reading," I murmured. I wanted to say, *No, when I wanted to talk, you were out with Melody.* She didn't ask twice. She never did.

I knew that calling me Manda signaled she felt a little guilty, but I had no intention of letting her off easy. We both had the tough, unforgiving gene. When I got tired, I turned off the light above my bed. I thought about the story. A woman learns that her father kidnapped her as a child to protect her from her alcoholic mother. I wondered whether I'd be mad at my dad for lying about my mother being dead, or if I'd be thankful that he put his life at risk to save mine. At that moment I wanted my dad to take me somewhere, anywhere, as long as it was away from her.

Melody came into our room and flung my wrap and sunglasses onto my bed. She flipped on the light next to her bed, putting it on the brightest setting before dropping her wet towel and bikini to the floor. I was about to curse her out when our parents started going at it again. The hotel walls were as thin as the ones at home.

"Amanda just doesn't listen . . . or think."

"Let it go, Susan."

"Don't tell me to let it go."

"She's been worked over enough today." The volume of the television went up. I guess Dad was attempting to save me from hearing her latest tirade.

"When will she learn?" The Captain carried on.

"C'mon. Christ, it was an accident."

"Turn that brain killer down. Please. I want to read. Some of us like to expand our minds."

"Okay, Ms. Smarty-Pants. Sorry this mere high school grad is only smart enough to rake in the dollars. Maybe with your guidance, our girls will be as accomplished as you one day."

"You know full well why I can't work full-time."

I remembered when The Captain was working. Everything at home was better, and not because of the money. She didn't obsess about me or my whereabouts as much. It seemed like she enjoyed her job, like she had a purpose outside of us.

"What keeps you handcuffed to the house?"

"Oh right, of course. You weren't around when Amanda was failing eighth grade. Or when she was turning into a juvenile delinquent."

"Right, you're so *right*," my dad said.

"What we should worry about is that Amanda's much more you than me. That's what we really have to worry about. Not whether either of them is as accomplished as I."

"If we're lucky, at least Amanda will stay that way, like me."

"Well, you can rest easy. Don't you worry . . . there's not a sliver of me in her body."

"Susan, shhhhh! . . . Keep your voice down," he snapped.

I lay there and let each of those words, *not . . . a . . . sliver . . . of . . . me . . . in . . . her . . . body*, seep like ice into my veins. I curled tighter, pulling my knees into my chest.

Dad turned the television up louder.

From her side of the room, Malady groaned, "See what you did? Again. I knew you would ruin our vacation—just like you do everything!"

"Shut up," I shouted back, wanting to reach across the space separating our beds and suffocate her.

"Couldn't you have at least waited a whole day before spoiling everything?"

"*Shut up,*" I repeated.

"Both of you be quiet in there," The Captain screamed from the other room. "Turn that damned TV down, Len. I'm tired and we have another five wonderful hours together in the car in the morning." The volume was lowered.

"God. This family sucks," Melody said, turning her back to me and pulling the covers over her head.

I couldn't sleep. I picked up my journal. As I listened to Melody's soft sniffling, I wondered if every family sucked like mine. If it weren't for the thought of Paul waiting for me, I probably would have thrown myself out of the car when we got back on the road.

4

After the pool incident I gave up wanting any relation-ship with my mother. I felt like a feather tackling a concrete wall, trying to get along with her. I couldn't get past how cold she had been when I obviously needed her. How she left me to be by myself after the most humiliating ex-perience of my life. No sympathy for you—Suffer In Silence, SIS. This was how The Captain grew up, and it seemed like another tradition she wanted to pass along to Melody and me.

> Your mind understands what you have been taught; your heart, what is true.

In the morning, when the three of them went down to the lobby for breakfast, I called Aunt Jen. "It's me. I only have two minutes."

"Hello to you too," she laughed. I could picture her warm espresso eyes.

I retold *Cruel at the Pool,* starting with how I could really understand why she says her period is her "bitch visiting." Aunt Jen felt terrible about the whole thing.

"Grandma Sturtz didn't show much sympathy for us when we were younger. I've told you how SIS was the mantra in our house."

"So then Mom *should* know how I feel."

"She does. Don't tell her I told you this, but when she was your age she got her period one night and soaked through the sheets and mattress. Our mom was so furious that she made your mom scrub everything until it was clean. I remember that day clearly. Your mother told me she felt dirty and stupid."

"Hello. She did the same thing to me. I hate her. And Melody," I said.

Aunt Jen was quiet for a minute. She sighed. "Don't say that. You don't hate your mom—it's your age. Trust me, it's a stage you're in."

"Trust *me,* I don't think it's a *stage.*"

"She loves you and wants what's best for you."

"What's best for me is to feel like I have a mother with a heart."

"She does, and I know you know that because yours is so big."

"Whatever. I'd better go before I get in trouble for keeping them waiting."

"Okay. But forget about the bitch. Your period, not your mother." She chuckled a little. "Seriously, she loves you. So do I."

"Whatever you say. Love you too."

"Call me as soon as you get to the condo."

When we hung up, I thought about something Gram, my dad's mom, once said: "You can tell a lot about a tree from the fruit it bears."

The only person my mother didn't seem cold and unsympathetic toward was her best friend, Marion. I had heard so many good stories from Marion about when she and my mother were young. How they always had each other, and "Thank God," because they didn't have much more than that. How they were inseparable—blood sisters. My mother always made comments that she was closer to Marion than she was to her own sister. That they protected each other and took care of each other and would do anything for each other.

I fantasized about traveling back in time, back to August 1991 in Verplanck, New York. As if in a movie, I look my mom up and find her there, hanging out with Marion at the local diner. They're teenagers, and I'm pretending to be a teenager in her time. My mission is to hand her that first fortune I got on the way to Myrtle Beach. Give her a little instruction on life.

Somehow I slip the little paper into her pants pocket. The moment before I am to be conceived, the slip of paper falls out onto the seat of my teenage father's car. He picks it up and hands it back to her. She reads *"The smart thing is to prepare for the unexpected"* to him. He pulls out a condom from his wallet and they continue kissing. And instead of being created, I'm dumped out the window in the CVS parking lot.

Mission completed—she goes on with her life, has fun with her friends, like it was before me. Instead of juggling babysitters and night classes, she goes away to college with Marion. They even room together, and my mom winds up being a freelance writer too. They coordinate trips to exotic places for their writing assignments. She travels the world instead of being here with me and Melody and the man she maybe never intended to marry.

I ran the fantasy a couple of times in my head, changing the version a little each time, obsessing about it, how it would have been better for her, how she would have been happier with her friend. Everything would have been different if not for their accident, if not for me.

Brittle Bond
I hope in another lifetime
You could be my mother again,
And I could go back on my mistakes
And I could blend with you
And you could mend the differences
And we could love and care for each other
In a world where fights between mothers and daughters
Are nonexistent

Where people are much more laid-back
But we can't change now
We can't give in
We have built a wall between each other
And we don't want to demolish our
Hard work constructing it
We have to fight
If we didn't . . . it already would be
In another lifetime.

8.2.07 by Amanda Sturtz Himmelfarb
on the way to Myrtle Beach

5

Shortly after we arrived at our condo, my mother attempted to "start fresh." She was in the middle of scrubbing the kitchen sink when I walked in.

"You're finished unpacking already?" she said, surprised. I could almost hear her saying, *But she usually operates in reverse*.

"Yeah," I said, plopping down on a stool at the kitchen bar.

"Yes."

I sighed.

"Amanda, I correct you so you speak properly. So you present yourself better."

I was in no mood. *Just leave me alone*, I wanted to say.

"I'd like to have a talk with you. I thought we might try something," The Captain said, moving on to the countertop in her systematic way: round and round four times to the right, and two smaller quick circles to the left. "I was thinking that, maybe, we might try to talk, *really* talk."

I fixated on the scrubbing, but I could hear her talking in the distance about establishing some guidelines and being honest. She stopped what she was doing and slid over a soft caramel-colored leather diary—a little bigger than a short paperback—with the word *Notebook* in darker brown embossed on the top. A cream grained-ribbon page marker dangled from the bottom.

"Thanks," I mumbled. Naturally, she forgot I already kept a journal.

"It's a little gift that I was saving for your birthday but forgot to give to you."

Like you forgot my birthday dinner? I thought.

"Sometimes when you write your feelings down, it's easier to express yourself."

I folded into myself. *Is she kidding? She doesn't have a clue about me.* I had this urge to scream at her, *Don't you remember my English teacher saying that I'm a talented writer? How for once you were happy with my grades and said, "I knew you could do it," when you got my report card that quarter?* I remembered; I had felt like I could fly.

I said nothing, though. I noticed how when my mother spoke to me she'd always shift her face at least twenty degrees away from mine, so that her eyes looked completely past me. It was like she was speaking into the air. I closed my eyes tight, squeezing out the pain, imagining myself in front of a podium with one solitary person in the audience—my mother.

Susan's Eyes

Your eyes are different from the ones
In the clichéd poems
They don't hold love in them
Or sparkle like a star
Your eyes aren't fragile, like a butterfly's wounded wing
Or nimble like a ballerina
Your eyes shatter glass
They peel the skin off an unworthy girl
The duo plans to conquer my "faulty behavior"
They hold me responsible . . . hold me down—
chaining me up to accusations
"If it weren't for you," they wince when
They catch other women wearing business suits
Your eyes don't look at me
Instead they look past me, through me as if I
were translucent as tracing paper
"If it weren't for her," they yawn
On unsteady nights.
Your eyes say what your mouth doesn't
Just as my pencil admits what I can't
Your eyes regret me.

8.3.07 by A.S.H.
1st nite Myrtle Beach

"I want to try to relate to you and remember what it was like to be a teenager." Her words brought me back to reality.

"Okay?" she asked.

"Okay, I guess." *How can you relate to me when there's not a sliver of you in my body?*

"Maybe you could even share some of what you write with me."

"Yeah. Um, maybe."

"Think about it."

She just didn't get it. Too little too late.

Who was I? she wanted to know. If she only knew how I thought about Paul when I used the back massager she had given me the year before, for my fourteenth birthday—*happy birthday to me*. If she only knew what Paul and I said to each other and the lies I made up about being experienced. If she knew even a tidbit of my thoughts, she'd deliver a version of the *your body is a temple and you have to honor it* lecture. It was funny how she had no idea that lots of girls in ninth grade and plenty in tenth let boys *enter their temples*.

I was certainly not showing her my writing or telling her anything. *Why should I?* I wasn't involved in drugs. I read five times as much as I was on the computer or watching TV. Still, The Captain acted like I was some delinquent.

She wanted to know what I think about, who I *am*? As if I would tip her off that my goal was to make Paul my first. As if I'd share what we had been IM'ing over the past year. I shared it all with my friends, though. Deanna had dared me to lose "it" to Paul. I wasn't sure if I was going to, but we were all willing to put money down that Deanna would if she were in my shoes. Of course, she'd already "been there, done that"—she'd even point out a guy in the hall who she'd "done." I guess once the bridge opens, all ships are free to sail through.

My mother thinks Deanna is a "floozy," a slut. She is. But I've known her for so long, I'd feel bad not being friends. I mostly ignored the way The Captain worked my friends over when she went into one of her tirades. She'd nitpick and strip them down, the way she eats food off a bone—gnawing and pulling and plucking every morsel of meat.

But I really couldn't take it when she'd crack on Paige. Besides being the one friend I can count on, Paige and I share a lot of interests—like trading great books. Ironically, this is something I used to do with my mom when she signed the three of us up for a parent-teen book club. I loved it, but Melody hated it. The Cap stopped taking us; I figured she felt it was a good idea for three but not two. I guessed she didn't want to be with just me. Though, once my mother and I had this intense conversation about human nature after reading Robert Cormier's *Tunes for Bears to Dance To*. It's still the best story I've ever read about evil, the extent to which it can live in someone and the amazing reach of it—one man's evilness literally invades and destroys this boy's soul.

Paige and I started swapping with *Stargirl,* and we've exchanged, like, thirty books since then. Sometimes they get to us, like *Olive's Ocean* did.

After reading that, Paige and I renewed our "blood

sisterhood," ceremoniously taking turns applying a lip gloss we stole from Sephora instead of pricking our fingers and smushing our blood together like we did back in third grade. We declared it our symbolic BFFL lip gloss and vowed never to take our friendship for granted. The day we performed our ritual in Paige's bedroom, her mom poked her head in, and we explained what we were doing. She thought it was cool.

"Love the creative older-girl version," she said.

"Yeah." Paige smiled back.

"Just don't share the same boyfriend in a few years when you redo your vows," she said, winking at me.

"Eww. Gross," we blurted at the same time.

Paige and her mother got even tighter after Paige's dad died. He had been a pilot for a private corporation, and his plane crashed when we were in eighth grade. It was a single-prop plane, and a fire had broken out in the engine. The whole plane went up in flames as it hit the ground, and Paige's dad and the two passengers were instantly killed.

Paige's mom fell into a deep depression and Paige was barely functioning. She stopped doing any work and was caught in school with a bottle of alcohol in her purse. She wasn't going to drink it, though—it was one of those little airline bottles from her dad's collection. The Captain heard about the school incident from Malady and assumed the worst. She also thinks Paige is a pothead, because one time she found a tiny bag of it in her purse, which my mother was digging into because she thought it was mine. Paige and I had tried it, but neither of us liked it. But The Cap still occasionally sniffs me and searches through my bag without permission. After the pot incident, *Perturbed over Herb*, The Cap threatened, "If I ever catch you smoking, including cigarettes, your social life will be nonexistent."

The shoplifting incident, *The Rift over the Lift*, did not help her view of Paige. We had decided to steal two tank tops. Mine was sticking out of my jacket when the Lord & Taylor security guard grabbed me. After the records got expunged with the help of Marion's lawyer friend, The Captain bought the exact tank I'd tried to lift from the store. Then she placed it on top of my other shirts and told me not to remove it, and not to unfold it. It was a relic that constantly resurfaced, the thing I'd have to see every time I opened my drawer.

What The Captain had said stuck with me. "Amanda, you're like a puppet controlled by an unimpressive cast of friends." I didn't think it would be wise to correct her and tell her the shoplifting was my idea.

> **To study a subject best,
> understand it thoroughly before.**

The Captain and me relating to each other, the two of us being like Paige and her mom, sharing secrets and not fighting, didn't seem possible. Changing my relationship with The Captain seemed as likely as my getting recruited by Harvard. The thing is, I was far from interested in either goal. My only interest was in hooking up with Paul.

6

Desperate

If he wants me
I can't say no
I can't fall back from the clouds to the
Ground floor
To the basement
And he seems to give me stairs upward
But I don't know
I'm scared
I would talk to you about it
If you weren't the one pushing me—
away.

8.4.07 by A.S.H.

The weekend was shot because Paul's cousins were staying with his family and they weren't leaving until Monday morning. I was bumming about not seeing him right away. The only benefit was that I'd get to improve my tan some more. With this in mind, I went down to the beach in my skimpiest shorts, the same shorts that caused *The Sin of Too Much Skin* when I'd worn them to school. I'd asked The Captain on my way out if they passed inspection. She sighed, then reluctantly nodded her approval. She knew I was wearing a pad. I assumed she'd wait another month to fight about tampons again.

I was lost in a book when she sat down on the lounge chair next to mine. "Isn't it beautiful here?" she asked.

"Yes," I said, not taking my eyes off the page.

"I can't believe I still haven't read that. I know it's supposed to be very good," she said.

"It is. I swapped Paige *Running with Scissors* for it." Mentioning Paige makes her groan, so I expected cutting comments.

"I'd like to read it when you're finished."

"Okay."

"You know, I brought a bunch of good books with me. You're welcome to them."

"Thanks, but I doubt that I'll like what you're reading," I said without thinking. I knew that she was trying to make up, but I was still mad. I knew I should let it go, but it was too hard.

"I love that you're such an avid reader, Amanda. I've always been a reader too. You've been devouring books since you were a baby," she said, looking out at the waves. I felt guilty that I was being so stubborn. At least she was trying. It just wasn't easy to let it all go—it was never easy for us.

"I'm glad we always have books in the house," I said, letting her in a little.

"Me too." She smiled and then rested her head back and closed her eyes.

It was nice sitting next to her—just the two of us, relaxing on the beach, even though all I really cared about anymore was seeing Paul.

The perfect opportunity to get together with Paul came when my parents made plans to meet their friends for dinner. I knew it would be a late night. My mom complained about not wanting to drive to some restaurant when it was "a perfectly good evening to grill and spend family time."

"We need time together too," Dad said. He came up behind her and kissed her. I guessed La-La Man also wanted to let go of anger.

"Fine, I'll go." The Captain sighed, smiling at my dad.

As soon as they left, I told Melody I was going to bed. When I felt the coast was clear, I slipped out my window.

> Many changes of mind and mood; do not hesitate too long.

The water was black. But in the waves you could see the whiteness of the foam; it reminded me of frothed milk on a hot mocha latte.

It was my going to be first time doing more than making out.

He was there waiting for me. I could see his white life-guard T-shirt clearly through the night. He looked perfect—tan, tall, messy blond surfer boy hair and blue eyes. He smiled. My heart hiccupped. I took my time—*Calm down, girl*—and strolled up to him, arms swinging, flip-flops looped around my thumbs. I was nervous, but thrilled with how cool and sexy I felt.

"I thought August would never come," he said, grabbing me close. It felt amazing to be in his arms. "Ready for some fun?"

"You have no idea," I said, holding his hand tightly. I wasn't sure whether I was more scared of what could happen with him, or of what The Captain would do to me if she caught us.

We held hands and walked in the direction of the life-guard chair. "I can't wait to be with you."

"Me too . . . I mean . . . uh, y'know." I giggled.

"To be with me too?" he laughed.

"Yeah," I told him.

"You sure about that? You don't sound like it." He squeezed my hand tighter.

"Yeah, I'm sure," I said, but as my feet sank into the sand, the truth was, I wasn't totally sure.

We climbed all the way up to the top of the lifeguard chair and Paul took a Myrtle Beach Town and Rec Department blanket out of his backpack and spread it on the damp wooden seat. Scents overwhelmed me: the salty ocean in his hair, his skin and the alcohol on his breath. He pulled out a flask. He handed it to me. "Ladies first." I took a sip.

"Whoa." It slid down my throat like lava.

"C'mon, take a bigger sip, chug some," he said. I did, taking two huge gulps, then another when it came back to me. We started to make out, our sticky lips full of heat.

He pulled me close, kissing deeper and twirling his tongue around mine, tasting like sea salt and my dad's scotch.

When he came up for air, he said, "I've been dying for this all year." I was worried I wasn't kissing good enough. I rolled my shoulders back and arched so he could see what I had. I acted like I did it to get a stretch, like I was unaware that this made my boobs shake slightly.

"Me too," I said, and for a second he looked lost. *Put under by the boobage.* "So how's it going with the lifeguarding?" I asked, hoping to figure out what I would do or say if he tried to go too far. I didn't want to say I had my period, because I know that grosses guys out.

"Amanda, I've been waiting, like, a year for you." He started kissing me harder.

His hands slipped under my halter, first rubbing my rib cage, and then unhooking my bra, causing a slight breeze of crisp air to hit my bare skin. I knew what was next, but that didn't prepare me for his hands gently cupping my boobs, and his thumbs pressing against my nipples and then squeezing them with his forefinger. I felt heat and tingles below. It was like having my knee tested for a reflex. Gentle squeeze. Whammo. Instant heat. I tried to regulate my breathing. The summer before, when Paul and I had first kissed, he had touched me a little, but it was *nothing like this*. I could hardly focus on any one thought: how far I should let him go, how I would stop him, what was maybe going to happen next. He seemed experienced, and I wondered if he could tell I wasn't, and if he'd realize I had lied about stuff. His hands were sure. He lifted my halter over my head and peeled my bra off my shoulders. I felt so exposed. His mouth brushed away from mine, trailing soft kisses first down my neck, then to my boobs. I arched toward him again, not meaning to this time.

I tried to say something, but his tongue was in my mouth—and then he started to move his hands up my legs. I had to stop him before he touched the pad. I kept thinking, *What should I say? What should I do? Should I tell him I'm being bitch-slapped? No. I should have prepared something to say for this. I should have prepared for the unexpected.* When his hands began pulling my skirt up, I blurted, "No, don't," and pushed his hands and then my skirt back down over myself. I grabbed my halter top and covered myself with it.

"What's wrong?" he said, totally not hearing me, moving his hands from my thighs, where I'd pushed them away, back to what apparently was his goal.

Obviously my no was not *no* enough.

"Stop. Please," I insisted, startling us both.

He stopped kissing me. "What's the deal?" he asked.

"I don't want to do that."

"What, are you kidding?"

"No. I'm not."

"Are you just a tease?"

"No!" I said, insulted.

"Then why would you build me up for a whole year, telling me how we would be together?"

"I want to, but just not tonight."

"*Unbelievable.*" He started to get up.

"Where are you going?" I asked, afraid I'd blown everything.

"Back. I have work in the morning."

"Paul, wait. It's just that—"

"That you obviously lied and you don't want to do anything?"

"Yes, I do." I clung to his shorts.

He was standing over me about to climb down from the top of the chair. If I hadn't had my period, I might have let him do whatever he wanted so I could get what I wanted. I wanted him to *want* me.

He stared at me with a look I'll never forget. "Don't go," I said, trying to avoid looking straight into his crotch. He stepped closer to me and grabbed my hand, pressing it gently on him. I felt the hardness of the wooden chair beneath me. I understood what he wanted. I wasn't sure if I could or how it would work. There wasn't a lot of room on the seat of the lifeguard chair. As if he read my mind, he leaned down and lifted my elbows, and I stood up. We kissed for a few minutes, hard and long. "I want you," he whispered.

"I want you too," I breathed back. Then he unbuttoned his shorts and pushed his boxers down. He moved the blanket under his bare ass as he sat down, then grabbed my hand, pulling me toward him. He rubbed my stomach. "You're so hot." Slowly, I knelt. The damp wood felt cold and slimy on my knees. He guided my face above *it* and pushed my head, and with it my mouth, over him. I started. He held my head there and all I wanted to do was pull it back. My jaw hurt. My knees hurt. I felt like I would gag and almost did a couple times. I was scared to death of what would happen if I had to continue another second. But I didn't want him to go. I didn't want him to think I was a tease or, worse, some dork. Himmel*fart*. *Stay with it*, I told myself. If I made him feel good enough, we would be together for the rest of the summer.

When it squirted in my mouth, I nearly vomited and an empty sensation ran through me. I didn't want to get upset or act strange. I had done it. I might as well collect my prize. Make the best of it.

Afterward, he said, "Wow. That was great. You're *good*." I didn't feel *good*; in fact, being *wanted* and being *good* had made me feel like a crumpled-up piece of trash.

Just Throw It Away
I am disposable—
No smile can illuminate me
No song can make me dance
There is no rhythm in my family

38

I cannot make harmony
With a voice that's belting a different tune.
I was not made for this
I may look like watercolor paint
But I cannot blend
I am oil paint
I stain
I am not right
I can only be me
I am disposable.

8.7.07 by A.S.H.

I needed to wash all the noise in my brain into the black waves. Push everything out of my head and make it neat again. Or at least into a space where I knew who I was.

7

We climbed down the chair and started heading back. Paul put his arm around my shoulder. He was telling me some story about this kid he'd had to give CPR to. I don't remember the details or how we got to that—maybe I wasn't listening. It just felt good having his arm around me, even though I could still taste him in my mouth. I started rationalizing. *So what? Isn't this what everyone does? I did what I had planned to do for a year—or at least, part of what I had planned.* We came to the wooden walkway that led from the beach to the locked gate of our development. The lights weren't on and it was really dark. Paul fumbled with his key card. "I can't get it in. I can't see." I took it from him. Running my fingers over it, I felt the smooth magnetic strip. "Got it," I said, slipping his card in the slot.

Paul pushed the metal gate open, leaned on it and gently pulled me against him. "You're good at everything, aren't you?" He was holding my arms gently at the wrists and bringing his chest toward mine.

"No, I'm not." I spoke softly, playing it.

I closed my eyes, feeling his tongue swirl around mine. He was making his way up my shirt when someone grabbed my shoulders from behind. I lost my balance and slammed against the hard walkway.

"What the fu—"

"AMANDA! Get up!" The Captain screamed. "Who's this?" She took a step toward us.

"Hey," he said.

"Hey," she sneered, full of contempt not only for Paul but for the expression, which totally annoys her. "*Hey* is for horses," according to the *Captionary*.

"Mom. Please," I said, getting up, my chest pounding.

"Don't you dare . . . *What's going on here?* Who's this boy?"

"He lives—"

"We've been looking all over the place for you!"

"I'm sorr—"

"Is that alcohol I smell? *Amanda*, were you drinking?"

"No, I . . ." Even though it was pitch black, I could still see her face.

"Don't you say another word, young lady. You'll have plenty of time to explain yourself!" She turned back to Paul in a fury. "She's fifteen!"

"Oh . . . um . . . I didn't know."

"Well, *y'know* now. Consider yourself informed!" my mother shouted.

"I . . . I'm sorry, m-ma'am," he stuttered. "I . . . I . . . didn't know." He looked baffled. His eyes darted between The Captain and me as if he were watching a Ping-Pong match.

"Where did you take her?"

"The . . . um . . ."

I looked at Paul, then back to my mother, seeing a desert mouse and a cobra.

She slithered closer to him. "Spit it out or I'll have the police get it out of you. *Now!*" she hissed, pointing her finger to the ground as if that was where he was supposed to deposit the info.

"For a walk on the beach," Paul mumbled nervously.

"With alcohol? How old are you?"

"Eighteen."

"Eighteen. Eighteen!"

My brain froze for a second, but then it struck me I should hightail my ass toward our condo. I had to get her away from Paul so he wouldn't see what a total psycho she was.

NOT HAPPENING.

I couldn't even plant my first getaway step on the ground. My ear was yanked back, and it rang with a deafening siren. I brought my hand up to cover my head. She grabbed my wrist, and I jerked it away. We were screaming, yelling, and

I lost track of time and space and everything. Through a dizzying haze I saw Paul backing up, a frightened deer caught in the hunter's trap. "Just go," I managed to say. Paul darted away into the night, without me. I wanted to die. I wished that I had drowned in the hotel pool.

My mother had a fistful of my shirt in her hand as she escorted me back to the condo. "You dare try to break away and you'll rue the day you were born."

My dad came out of the back door as we approached. "What are you doing?" he called out. "Stop!"

"She's going to tell us every dirty detail."

"So you can tell people what a dirty little girl I am?" I shouted, trying to head inside.

My dad yelled, "Amanda, go to your room now."

"I'm not finished here," The Captain snapped.

"I can't take this. I can't hear this right now." I put my hands over my ears, trying to block her words.

"Too damn bad. Really, Amanda—do you really believe he likes you for *who* you are, not *what* your body has to offer?"

"God forbid someone could want me," I seethed.

"Oh ... of course, play the victim now ... poor Amanda—someone please feel sorry for me."

"Susan." La-La Man turned on The Captain and shot her a look, and then he turned to me. "Amanda, go upstairs." I ducked to avoid a slap The Cap tried to land on me by coming around his back.

I ran up to my room, shutting myself in. I should have

been home earlier or begged Melody to cover for me. Again, I hadn't prepared for the unexpected. Curled up on my window seat, I listened to their screaming.

"Apple tree, Susan. Hitting begets hitting."

"Don't you ever say that to me. You're like *your* mother—superior with no basis."

"Keep my mother out of this. I'm talking about how you treat Amanda. It's got to stop. No matter what she does, she shouldn't be hit."

"What's got to stop is *your* judging *me*. You have no idea what it's like. *No idea*. You get to prance in here, like her, in your own world, and be a parent when it's convenient for you. I'm here *day in* and *day out*. You don't have any idea what she's like."

"I work my ass off to support you and the girls, in case *you* haven't noticed. You lost control, and we all know how much you hate that. I don't think you realize how much you're becoming—"

"Shut up. I am *not* my mother. You don't say that to me, *ever*. Or I swear to God the next time you do, I'll walk out the door forever. And let me tell *you* something, *Len*. Alone at night on the beach with an eighteen-year-old boy is not acceptable. She will *not* be allowed to gallivant around, and I won't tolerate your condoning it."

"It's not about condoning anything. It's about how you need to handle things by talking, not with corporal punishment."

"Since when are you the expert? How many times have you sat with that girl and helped with her homework?"

"You mean *our daughter?*"

"Yes. How many times have you been to a school conference to see what's going on with her? Once? How many swim meets have you attended? If I have to slap her to prevent her from making a mistake, I *will*."

"You mean like your mother?"

"You bastard. Sorry I can't be perfect like you *and* your mother. Put *'I'm sorry I couldn't be perfect'* on my gravestone, okay?"

"I'm sorry we all have to pay for your parents' mistakes. And, by the way, again, *my* mother has nothing to do with this. My parents took us in when yours wouldn't."

"Aren't they the best?" she sneered.

"They helped get me where I am, working hard as hell to make sure my children have a future. And, FYI, I have a say in how we raise *our* children."

"You *raise* cattle; children are *reared*."

"Really? Well, *you* were *reared* by the Bitch of the Universe," he seethed.

"Are you calling me a bitch?"

"You're not Mary Effin' Poppins."

"I can't stand you," she screamed even louder than before, and I jumped, the way I do every time she slams a door shut.

8

In dreams we
awaken realities.

Somehow Paul and I arrange to meet at the head lifeguard chair again. In the dark I walk through the sand, my feet sinking farther with every step, like quicksand is sucking me down. I don't know how, but I manage to make it to the ladder. I smell the salt of the ocean. He smiles. My heart melts. I want him to pull me close, to feel his strong chest, muscular arms. I feel his desire for me. We're kissing; he's stroking my hair. "I really, really like you, Amanda," he says. "I like you," I say. "You do?" he says, placing his hands on my shoulders. As he's pressing me down, I'm startled awake.

I realized I was dreaming and sat up.

I immediately thought of *A Separate Peace*. It was on the tenth-grade summer reading list and I had just finished it. I found the part:

> Until now, in spite of everything, I
> had welcomed each new day as
> though it was a new life, where
> all past failures and problems were
> erased, and all future possibilities
> and joys open and available,
> to be achieved probably
> before night fell again.

Gene realizes that Phineas can't ever remake himself. That problems don't go away overnight. Here it was the morning after, and I realized the same thing. Sleep wouldn't change what went on the night before—like the sun, my angst would reappear every morning.

I called Paige and told her everything that had happened with Paul and The Captain's ambush. Then I mentioned *A Separate Peace* and my dream about Paul. "I wish I could erase what happened last night," I cried to her.

"I know. There's plenty I wish I could erase. Stuff I'll never have the chance to fix." I knew she was talking about how she'd fought with her dad the morning of his plane crash.

Some things just can't be fixed.

9

> **Keep in close touch with what
> your competition is doing.**

My cell phone was confiscated the morning after *Commotion at the Ocean* and The Captain instituted new rules. The whole disaster set off a string of fights between my parents. They argued over my night with Paul, including the way The Captain and I had fought. Listening to them made me sick.

"She's grounded through the weekend, and for the duration of the trip, she's not going *anywhere* unsupervised."

"We're on vacation, for chrissake. Can't we enjoy it?"

"And how would you like us to do that *now*? Maybe we should act like nothing happened and let her have sex with that boy."

"I'm not saying that. She'll be with one of us. You're impossible. . . . The apple . . ."

48

"I told you, Len, if you say that to me one more time . . . Why do we even go to counseling? You don't even try. Dr. Rubin says, 'Think before you speak,' but you never can, can you?"

"I guess not."

"You know that comment is a trigger for me."

"There's a lot that triggers you," Dad said. He stormed out of the condo.

During the War at the Shore, The Captain and La-La Man barely spoke to each other except to exchange dirty looks and quick yes-or-no answers, and the family basically divided into camps. I avoided The Captain and spent most of my time hanging around with my dad, while Melody and The Captain were off lounging at the beach, playing tennis or working on the candle-lighting speech for Melody's bat mitzvah. I'd be upstairs in my room and hear them laughing about the rhymes they'd come up with. Or discussing Melody's hairstyle for the party.

Despite my humiliation, I wanted to be with Paul again. I kept thinking about ways that I could sneak out and see him. I didn't think it would be so bad if I did what he wanted again or even more since I wouldn't have to worry about my period. But the few times I snuck into my parents' bedroom to text Paul from my confiscated cell phone, he didn't answer. Getting ice cream with Daddy was so not how I had imagined my summer. It was so not what I had planned.

One afternoon, walking with strawberry slurpies, Dad suggested we go down to the tennis club and watch Melody and Mom play. Besides, I hate tennis, but we didn't have anything better to do.

My mother and Melody had been keeping a running score since June. They're both really competitive. I guess the way I am with swimming. I lived for the day that I'd beat Courtney.

We walked into the club and went one flight up to the seating area overlooking the courts. The Captain was slamming a serve over to Melody. It hit the corner of the service box and Melody made an amazing return, though popping the ball up to The Cap. She nailed the overhead, whacking it down and sending it straight up in the air. Melody was all confused. She started backing up, trying to see where the ball was coming down, and somehow in pulling her racquet quickly back, Melody hit herself in the head. We heard her yell "Owww" through the break in the safety glass and then watched The Cap run over. I could see my mother asking if she was okay and then rubbing Melody's head, and the two of them started cracking up. Melody reenacted the scene with her racquet and my mom threw her head back, laughing like a hyena.

Disgusted, I told my dad I wanted to walk home by myself. I wanted to look for Paul.

"No. I'll walk you back," Dad said.

So instead of Paul, I walked on the beach with La-La Man. Five days had passed and I still hadn't seen Paul again, not even from a distance. I didn't know what he thought about us anymore.

10

The decision to "just leave!" was made exactly two weeks from the day we arrived. Even though we'd planned to leave a few days early because of Melody's bat mitzvah, The Captain demanded we head back home even earlier. A random fight over my mother's wedding band was the "final straw."

We had just finished dinner on the porch, and my mother was washing the dishes. My father started first. "That's nice—leave your ring I sacrificed my college education for next to the drain."

My mother pointed to the mound of suds coming out of the sink. "I'm not sure if you noticed, but I'm washing the dishes."

I was standing stiffly at attention with a towel, waiting for the next dripping dish. Dad looked at me.

"Why isn't Melody helping?" he demanded. Melody was stretched out on the couch, watching TV.

"What did I do?" Melody moaned.

The Captain said, "Nothing. You didn't do anything wrong." Then she turned toward my dad. "I don't think it's a wise idea to use the girls as pawns."

"I'm using them as pawns? Isn't that what Dr. Rubin would call a projection?" She threw the sponge on the counter and walked out, slamming the sliding glass door behind her. The Captain did a lot of door slamming, even though when I did it, she took my bedroom door off for a week so I'd remember never, ever to do it again. *She's so hypocritical,* I thought. La-La Man wasn't going to let this one go. He followed her out to the porch, the door screeching against the tracks as *he* slapped it shut. We could hear their muffled voices. A second later she opened the door and stuck her head back inside to yell, "Girls, pack up your things. We're heading back home in the morning. With or without your father." Then she slammed it shut *again* and walked off toward the beach.

La-La Man slid the door back open, stepped inside and turned back to yell to her, "Fine with me. Who needs vacation when work is ten times less stressful? I can be ready to go tonight." Then he slammed the door yet again.

He marched over to Melody. "Help your sister finish the dishes," he said, and then he went back outside, La-La Man making *his* getaway to the porch.

While we did the dishes, Melody told me about her friend Kelly, whose dad had moved out last May.

"She said it was a relief not to hear her parents fighting anymore, but her house has become deadly quiet and lonely," Melody said, rubbing the inside of a glass in circles until it squeaked. "Kelly told me that feeling depressed beats out feeling nothing." Melody shrugged and placed the glass in the cupboard the way The Captain liked—neatly lined up, orderly.

"I know exactly what Kelly means." I'm not the type to survive feeling nothing; I'm the type who feels everything. Aunt Jen thinks being über-emotional, oversensitive, is my blessing and curse. I didn't have the force field that Melody had managed to surround herself with.

"Do you think they'd actually do it?" she asked, looking down at me, already two inches taller. She rubbed the space between her brows. Back and forth. Rub. Rub.

"I don't know." I'd been thinking a lot about them getting divorced. All they seemed to do was pick, fight and scowl at each other until one of them walked out, into another room, or like this time, literally out the door.

"I think they might."

"If they do, I'm living with Dad," I said. I handed her a plate to dry, and she handed it back to me, showing the food still on it. I rewashed it and handed it back. "Stop twisting your sneaker. I hate that sound, and you're making *me* nervous," I said.

Funny thing was, she was more competent (if grades measured this), but I was the one who coped better with disappointment.

"You *should* be nervous."

"You shouldn't tell me what I should be."

"Why did you have to sneak out with Paul, anyway?" She was making faster drying circles on the plate.

"I wanted to have a good time like any normal person," I said.

"If you're so normal, why are they always fighting over you?" She slapped the plate on top of the others and grabbed the next one out of my hands.

Here we go. One minute about to console each other, the next attacking. Put on the Band-Aid, then rip it off later, taking skin and hair with it.

"Me? Why did you tell Mom you didn't know where I was in the first place, huh? Who are you, Benedict Malady?"

"Shut up. Don't call me that."

"Okay, Benedict Melody."

"Yeah, like it's my fault. Like they wouldn't have checked to see if you were here when they got home. Everything is always everyone else's fault except yours."

"Right."

"You're the traitor. We made a pact to get along, be flexible. Not do anything to make them fight."

"Blah, blah, blah."

"You're such a loser, Fart Face."

"Yeah, *I'm* the loser. FYI: You caused this. If you hadn't

told them I was out when they called, they would've gotten home *after* me. And *whatever* I am, at least I'm not a pathetic preppy dork like you."

"You're right, you're just pathetic."

She threw her dish towel at me, grabbed the portable DVD player from the living room and stomped up to her room, slamming her bedroom door shut. I was sick of all the slamming.

> **Anger is the cover of sadness.**

My father was sitting on the porch steps, looking out into the storm that seemed to come out of nowhere. I came up behind him.

He didn't turn to look my way; he just kept peering into the sheets of rain. "Go call Paige before Mom comes back," he muttered. "Your cell phone is in her night table drawer. But make sure you're packed up to leave in the morning. Tell Melody to do the same."

"I'm sure she already is."

"Well, don't you be the one we're waiting on."

"Okay. Sorry, Dad."

"Don't be."

Paige's mother answered. "Hi, Amanda," she said in her familiar, inviting voice.

"Hey. How are you?" I asked.

"Fine, thanks. How's Myrtle Beach?"

"Okay."

"Okay? You don't sound very convincing," she said. Her warm voice made the lump in my throat swell.

"Oh, I'm just tired."

"I'll get Paige. Hold on."

"Hi. I was just thinking about you. I've got to tell you something," Paige said when she picked up.

"What?"

"Wait. First, how are you?" she asked.

"Same. Still in trouble. Haven't seen or spoken to Paul, and now we're leaving tomorrow."

"That sucks."

"Yeah, I know. I guess I waited all year for twenty lousy minutes."

"Yeah. Well not many guys would come back for more after getting a taste of The Captain."

"I guess not."

"Unless it was for a taste of The Cap's daughter?" We laughed.

Paige continued. "Look, if he didn't like you, he wouldn't have kept in touch with you for a whole year."

"How do you know? Maybe he just wanted to make sure he was locked in for some August sex and really couldn't give a crap—"

"I doubt that."

"Now I won't even get a chance to say goodbye."

"That sucks. But I'm glad you'll be back."

"Home will be better than being trapped here."

"Don't be so excited to see me."

"You know what I mean. So, what were you going to tell me before?"

"Mom and I went downtown and . . . I got my belly button pierced."

"I want to do that! Did it hurt?"

"Like hell," she groaned, "and it's sore, but it's so worth it."

I could hear her mother in the background. "What is your mother saying?"

"She said that she wishes her belly were flat enough to get hers pierced, but thanks to me, it's flab city."

I laughed a little. "The Captain would never let me. I'll have to wait until I'm eighteen or God knows how old."

We talked for a few more minutes until I heard The Captain coming. Then I hung up and got ready for early evacuation.

11

I managed to text Paul again when my mother came back and was in the shower. "leaving 2morrow. can u walk to corner of breezeway and chester to say bye?" He sent back: "cant. out w friends. srry." I wondered if he realized I meant I was leaving right away so, I texted again, "im leaving 2morrow." Nothing.

Fast and Far Away
What happens when
All the things you count on turn
Dark?
And you see your shadow doing things
It's not supposed to?
The winds gaze at you,

Breathing cold gusts at your neck.
Emptiness.
They have seen it before.
What happens?
You run.
No matter what—
You run.
You run
Always because once you stop,
You are
Lonely.

8.17.07 by A.S.H.
in the car on the way home

The picture with Paul became undeniably clear after we arrived back in New York. I tried IM'ing him the minute I got up to my room, before The Cap took my computer away. I typed, "r u on?" Still no response. Even days after, in the snippets of time I'd get secretly using Dad's laptop, I tried to contact him. I could tell he was online, but he never wrote back. Finally he blocked me. No one had ever blocked me before. Like my blank screen, I felt empty.

I steered clear of The Captain. It was a continuation of Myrtle Beach. I moved in and out of rooms, anything to avoid crossing paths. She avoided me too, both of us uncomfortably comfortable being ships that pass in the night. Every day she'd leave a list of chores on the kitchen table—

weed garden, clean hallway bath, sweep garage, etc. I'd check them off, leaving the note out for her inspection. The Cap was big on actions speaking louder than words, so I did my tasks, left my pencil marks, and said nothing.

Melody got herself into a full-day tennis program. When she'd get home, she and The Captain would work on seating arrangements, flowers and other final details for the bat mitzvah. My mother seemed excited about all of it. She and Melody went crazy over the stupidest things, like center-pieces.

Dad wasn't around much. He had been working later than usual since we got back from vacation, and he had plans to leave soon on some big business trip. I spent the evenings in my room, reading and occasionally writing.

So I barely cared when The Captain took Melody into the city to do last-minute fittings on her dress, see a show and stay overnight as a birthday present. Miss Suck-up said that all she wanted to do was spend time with Mom. I pictured Malady bouncing for joy, putting on a preshow for our mother when they got their tickets to *Wicked*, the only show *I* was dying to see besides *Spring Awakening*. Paige's mom had gotten *Spring Awakening* tickets as a birthday gift for me, but The Captain made me say "No, thank you" after she'd read that they simulated sex onstage. My birthday consisted of Gram, Gramps and Aunt Jen coming over for cake and ice cream. My mother promised to do something special with me, but that never happened. And then here she was, celebrating Melody's birthday before mine, though mine was back in May. The implication was clear.

In the end, The Captain and Malady's going away worked out well because Dad let Paige sleep over. Paige and I ate junk food and watched movies all night. She was just what I needed. She talked me through my latest case of the blues. "Anyone who doesn't appreciate you doesn't deserve you," Paige said.

I loved Paige for saying that but I wasn't buying. "No guy's going to want to go with me for just my sparkling personality. But now that I have some experience, I'm gonna use it."

"You're more than your bubble butt, girl. Just make sure they like you for you."

After Paige left but before Melody, The Captain and Marion came back, I decided to be the better person and work on the party favors.

I figured I'd surprise my mother and put the "Melodious Evening" giveaways into the gift bags. But there were *9.1.07* sweatpants, *Melody* baseball caps and different-color Frisbees. I hadn't realized that the sweatpants were all different sizes and that certain colored hats and Frisbees were supposed to be in the bags of the same color, to be coordinated later with seating at a matching-color table. At my bat mitzvah we gave all the kids, whether boy or girl, a CD that I burned. My simple slipup created "another Amanda fiasco."

The Captain flipped out when she came into the den and saw that I had emptied everything out of the boxes and was randomly putting the items into the bags. "Oh no. No. No. No. This is all wrong."

"What?" I said. "I'm filling the gift bags."

"Why'd you touch my stuff?" Malady whined. "You're such a loser."

"Melody. Stay out of it," my mother said.

"Well, she is," Malady said.

"Shut up," I said.

"Both of you be quiet," The Captain shrieked. She grabbed her hair in two bunches as if she wanted to pull it out. "First of all, it's not supposed to be any pants in any bag. Didn't you see this list? This is what needs to be cross-referenced to get the correct items in the correct bag." She was waving the list at me.

"Oh."

"Amanda, that's why there are different colors. Boys and girls, different sizes too," The Cap explained in her typical *How-to for Dummies* way.

"Duh!" Malady said.

I shot her a look.

"Last warning, Melody." The Captain turned to me. "Sometimes, Amanda, your lack of help is better than your help." She probably would have gone off into a bigger tirade if Marion hadn't been with her. Marion was looking pretty uncomfortable.

"I'm sure we can fix this in no time," Marion said as she kneeled down on the floor to help The Captain undo my work and put the giveaways into organized piles so the bags could be restuffed Captain-style—efficiently and without error.

"Sorry for trying to help. I won't ever do it again," I muttered.

Marion looked up at me sympathetically.

"I suggest you change your tone. If only you had thought before you . . ." The Captain didn't finish her sentence. She just stuffed things in the bags harder. I picked up the list, and Melody snatched it out of my hands.

"Amanda, please. Melody, you too. Let Marion help me get this done." I dropped the Frisbee I was holding in my hand and went upstairs.

> You attempt things that you do not plan, because of your extreme stupidity.

12

The night of Melody's bat mitzvah made *Botched Bags* look "like a pimple on an elephant's ass," as Aunt Jen would say. The hairdresser my mother hired was an idiot. She put my hair up way too loosely. By the beginning of the cocktail party, the bun was already falling down because I did this wild dance competition on the kids' side of the room. Balancing my hair with one hand and holding a drink in the other, I spotted The Captain by the buffet table and rushed over to get help with my bun. I felt my gown being pulled from underneath me and heard the sickening sound of ripping fabric. The tip of my sandal had gotten caught up in my hem. In that moment of horror, when I knew I was going down, I instinctively held my virgin strawberry daiquiri up and as far away from my dress as I could. As I went sprawling through the crowd, it parted like the Red Sea. Standing in the middle was The Captain, like a deer in the headlights, in her cream chiffon Chanel, a shrimp roll halfway to her mouth. Needless to say, my bright red frozen drink that I successfully kept off my own dress splattered all across The Captain's. It instantly soaked in like red Magic Marker on paper towel, bleeding out and down the whole front of the dress.

While one of the waiters helped me off the floor, the rest of the crowd gathered around my mother. "For our next act . . . ," Dad joked. He grabbed a cocktail napkin from the bar and offered it to her.

My mother looked at him, then to the napkin, and then to me. She hurried away, saying nothing. I went after her. "Sorry, sorry. It was an accident. Please don't be mad." She kept going. We made quite a procession—Dad, Gram and Aunt Jen were following me following The Captain. Melody was still in the kids' cocktail area, oblivious to the crisis unfolding. Aunt Jen looked over at me, concerned.

"You can barely notice it," La-La Man tried to tell my mother.

"Are you kidding me?" she yelled, snatching her dress away from Gram, who was trotting along and dabbing uselessly.

"I'm sorry," I said again.

"Stop saying sorry," she snapped.

"It's okay, Amanda. It was an accident," Aunt Jen said, putting her arm around me.

"Jennifer, do you always have to tell her 'It's okay'?"

"Susan, she spilled something. She didn't put a knife in your back." Aunt Jen pulled me closer.

"I need some room." The Captain whipped her head around at me. "I can *always* count on you, Amanda."

"Susan, my God," Aunt Jen said.

Dad was steaming too. "She feels bad, for chrissake."

"*Leave—me—be.* All of you, go," she gritted out, rushing into the bathroom.

We went back to the party. My mother, wearing my dad's tux jacket, ignored me for the rest of the night.

> **Out of sight but
> NOT out of mind.**

The morning after, The Captain came into my room and woke me up.

"I need you to come with me to drive Marion to the airport."

"Why?"

"One, because I said so. Two, Marion is taking an international flight and has to be at the airport two hours early. I need you to stay with the car when I go in."

"What about Bat Mitzvah Beauty?"

"She stayed up late opening presents. And your snide remark is not appreciated."

"Well, that's really fair."

"Amanda, please. You're going to start with me after last night?"

"Fine," I huffed.

"No hour shower."

Actually, I didn't mind Marion. She came up from the city every month or so and she was pretty nice to talk to. She'd ask questions about me that weren't deadly like the school-related ones adults usually ask. Besides, I hadn't heard yet about the freelance writing assignment she was heading off to do.

On the way to the airport, my mother said, "Marion, I hate that you'll be gone for so long. You're my rock."

"It's only six months," Marion told her. "Maybe you'll have to plan a trip to Vietnam?" She turned and smiled at me in the backseat. She was dressed all in black, and it made her pale skin stand out even more.

I caught my mom looking at me in the rearview mirror.

"Marion, your gift to Mel was too generous."

"Don't be silly."

"Well, I hope you won't be behind with work because of me."

"Not at all. Would I ever miss a Himmelfarb event? I'll be in time for the big banquet."

"You can wear what you wore last night. It was stunning," my mother said. "You're getting too thin, though."

"Yeah, maybe."

"I know someone who won't ever be wearing *her* dress again."

"I'm sure the cleaners will get that stain out," Marion said.

"Don't put money on it."

Marion reached back and patted my leg.

"I only heard, 'Mooooom! My *bu—un!*' Over a single piece of hair," The Captain said to no one in particular.

"I said I'm sorry." I spoke to the window.

Marion turned around to me again. "Forget it. It's over." But it wasn't. It never would be. This was just another mess—*The Mess on the Dress.*

There were too many cops at the airport for my mother to double-park and go in, so she pulled up to the curb, put the car in park and sighed. Marion handed her a small box. "Here. It's that time." She smiled. My mother opened the card and began to read out loud. " 'Susan, you're always saying I'm your rock . . .'

"You are," my mother said in a small voice. She kept reading, but only to herself. She bent her head and made little *aw* sounds. Then she opened the box. Hanging on a black leather cord was a beautiful pearly-grayish stone shaped like a rock.

"Marion. You shouldn't have. This is so . . ." Her voice cracked.

"Don't cry on me now. . . . Here, let me help you." Marion fastened the necklace behind her neck.

My mother leaned forward and looked at it in the mirror. "It's gorgeous."

"That's really, really beautiful," I said.

"It's cool, right?" Marion smiled at me.

When my mother and Marion hugged, I could see the side of The Captain's face. Her eyes were tearing. She held on to Marion, and her body shook a bit. It was awkward to be right there—this was something I had *never* seen, not even when The Captain's mother had died five years ago.

She might have cried at the funeral had she gone, but she didn't. None of us did, except Aunt Jen.

"C'mon. You're supposed to be the tough one. Don't get me started."

"I'm not so tough."

Oh yes, you are. You are, you are, Cap-i-tan, I wanted to say.

We all got out of the car, and I helped get Marion's bags from the trunk.

"Thank you, sweets." She gave me a warm hug. "Listen, you better set up that e-mail address for your mother."

"I will. Tonight."

"I think you're terrific, Amanda—you really are unique."

"Yeah, right," I said.

"I know I'm right," she said, giving me another tight hug.

The Captain had gone to get a porter. I couldn't believe how choked up she seemed. I had noticed Marion was being the stronger one, although in their conversations, it always seemed like my mother was the one giving the advice. Maybe it was because she wasn't married and didn't have much family anymore.

When I went to get into the front seat, I caught one last glimpse of Marion, and she waved at me, smiling big. I wished my mother could be more like her—why couldn't Marion have been the one to get pregnant with me and not my mother? Then, as I slid into the front seat, I felt guilty for wishing that. Watching my mother watch her friend leave, I was sad for her. As her eyes followed Marion, her only friend, through the doors of the terminal, I could feel how much

The Captain wished she were the one flying to some far-off place.

If Paige were leaving for six months, I would be totally devastated. At least once a month my mother stayed overnight at Marion's. After she'd come home, she seemed to be relaxed and happier. She called these her "resuscitation days." I looked forward to these Friday or Saturday nights too—my resuscitation nights; it meant I could have Paige over without The Captain on my back.

Looking over at my mother, I really felt sorry for her for being how she was. For not having other friends. For being angry so often. It was like she didn't like her life. I felt bad for her for being so tough. I'd never really thought about it until then, but it seemed like being upset was harder on her than on other people. Like sadness was almost *more* painful *because* she was so tough.

"Six months isn't that long," I said. I knew I couldn't fill the passenger seat quite the way Marion did.

She didn't respond.

"Maybe we can go visit."

"You don't understand, Amanda."

"I'm just saying, you know, people say 'time flies,' well, before you—"

"Amanda, I need to concentrate on the road." She stared straight ahead without saying another word. A few times I made a comment about a house or another car. She stuck with silence.

When we walked in, my dad started right away with some

conversation he'd had with a business friend at Melody's bat mitzvah. Dad was going to be buying the inventory of some company and this was going to mean big business for him, and he went on and on until finally my mother said, "Len, I just dropped Marion off at the airport and I don't have the head for your success right now."

La-La Man quietly picked up his laptop and a pile of papers off the kitchen table. As he passed my mother, my dad noticed the necklace she was wearing.

"Where did you get the necklace?" he asked.

"Marion," she said, touching the stone.

"You like it?" he asked.

"Why?"

"No. I just wanted to know, so just in case I'm near any woods I can find a nice rock and some string and make you one." His chuckle hung in the air.

She gave him a look that could have turned *him* to stone. She glanced at me before going upstairs. I might have said something to defend her, to tell my dad what the rock meant, but she didn't deserve any pity after the way she'd treated me in the car. Plus, she'd made me out to be such an idiot in front of Marion.

Later she asked me to set up her screen name. Mrs. Efficiency was tech-challenged. I taught her how to write, send and read e-mail. I know it was wrong, but when she wasn't looking, I selected *Remember Password*, suspecting she'd be writing to Marion about what a difficult daughter I am, or gloating about Melody's perfect grades and how she may be Harvard-bound. I know my customer.

71

13

Subject: No Subject

Date: 9/3/2007 4:25:34 PM Eastern Standard Time

Sent from: Ssturtz@aol.com

To: Mardor@conde.org

Marion—

I hope you ended up sleeping on the flight.
How's Vietnam? I want pictures and descrip-
tions as soon as possible. Everything is rel-
atively status quo—Amanda and I are fighting.
She's a giant sponge, sucking the life out of
me. Jennifer and I had another fight about her
too. All these years later, she is still the
biggest pain-in-the-ass younger sister. Only
the issues have changed. It must be nice to be

the doting aunt and not worry about the end re-
sult. Anyway, school begins in a few days. I
hope I can survive another year. Counting this
one, only three more to go before college.
Did I tell you that Len is still angry that I
caused a scene in front of his precious mother
at the bat mitzvah? Or how not being the center of attention anymore has presented itself
in Melody as a sore throat and stomachache?
Oh, joy. You know how nurturing is not in my
DNA.
~S

Subject: RE: No Subject
Date: 9/4/2007 6:38:52 PM Eastern Standard Time
susan,
so tired. long trip. finally settled.
cute pied-à-terre with this great european pa-
tio. wish you could see it.
again great job with the bat mitzvah. beautiful night—that should be your takeaway. separate it from the dress. you know this.
xoxo, marion

Subject: RE: RE: No Subject
Date: 9/4/2007 10:05:52 PM Eastern Standard Time
Mar—
Thanks. But I didn't store a great memory. It's

depressing when I think about it. All the effort and money and I was miserable. I'm sure Amanda thinks I was overdramatizing. She doesn't recognize it's her carelessness and lack of thought process once again. Whatever I do or try to do doesn't seem to work out. Look how much time I put into the bat mitzvah. Look how it ended. Everyone is mad at everyone else—Len, Amanda, Melody, my mother-in-law, Jennifer. It's so frustrating. Imagine, my mother was only concerned with her rum and Cokes and Wheel of Fortune! And then her detox days. She certainly didn't try to create special memories or make quality family time. The truth is, I'm not even sure quality anything matters, especially with Amanda and me. It ends up being the exact opposite. I try. I just don't think she does. Melody isn't perfect, but at least she doesn't cause me so much grief.

Missing you,

~S

> **There is great ability in knowing how to conceal one's ability.**

The night before school started, The Captain gave me this whole lecture about not using the computer until homework was done and how I'd have no Friday night plans until all weekend homework was finished. Now that I was entering tenth grade, my "priorities should be studying and more studying." Melody was watching a movie in the den, not a part of any lecture because she's just the best.

"I'm not going to eat, breathe and sleep schoolwork. I'm not living for studying," I snapped.

"Amanda, why can't you understand that I'm looking out for your future?"

The louder we got, the higher Melody raised the volume. She was told to turn it down. She barely did, and The Captain went berserk. "Turn it off *now*."

"Why do I get punished for her stupidity?" She stomped up the stairs.

"Please. Enough!" The Captain yelled to her, turning her attention back to me. "Well, you better get a grip, because these grades will go on your transcript, young lady."

"So?" I put my hand on my hip and broke Rule #502: no rolling your eyes. My big *who cares* look.

" 'So?' 'So?' That's brilliant. Shrug and roll your eyes. Brilliant."

"Thank you." I smirked.

"Don't you dare get sarcastic. You don't have that luxury. Really, Amanda, don't you have any goals in life? Do you have a clue how competitive it is out there? Don't you want to get into *any* college?" She was starting to get really worked up.

"You went to college. What are your goals?" I shocked myself with this, but I was at a point where I no longer cared about being in trouble.

She went to grab my arm and I backed away. "The nerve. Who do you think you are?" Her hands were clenched.

"I'm just saying you're a housewife. What if that's what I want to be—just a housewife? And a mother?"

"*Just.*"

"Yeah."

"It's 'yes,' for the hundred millionth time. I don't know why I even bother sometimes. Why do I dedicate my life to you when this is what I get?"

To say she wigged wouldn't even scratch the surface— *Slayed over Grades* again. She began screaming and waving her hands around like a madwoman. She completely lost it. She came at me with the *Better Homes and Gardens* magazine she was holding. I moved away, but she still ended up partially whacking me with it, giving me wicked paper cuts. My arm looked like an angry cat had scratched me.

I screamed at her, "GET AWAY!" And she screamed back, "GET AWAY? YOU GET AWAY FROM ME!" We withdrew to our corners, our rooms. She slammed her door and then I slammed mine. I couldn't take any more. *Cruel at the Pool, Commotion at the Ocean, The Myrtle Beach Massacre, Botched Bags, The Mess on the Dress* and The Captain's nasty e-mails about me had already made me consider never speaking to her again. I wanted to shut myself off from the whole world and never hear The Captain's voice again.

Silence

Silence is my friend,
My enemy.
In the summer she is at my tree,
My special tree,
Waiting for me in the sun.
She is greedy.
Sometimes she tears at me,
While I want to stay surrounded by sound.
Oh, the sweetness of noise.
Not voices shouting,
Screaming words sharp as knives,
But singing.
I am with her now
Silence's
Cold, harsh voice tears me
But she is keeping me company.
Silence is my secret,
My hideaway from anger and fights.
She helps and haunts,
She knows,
She fears,
She feels
Everything
which is nothing
unless you have
Silence to base it on.

9.5.07 by A.S.H.

77

Subject: RE: RE: RE: No Subject

Date: 9/5/2007 6:32:32 AM Eastern Standard Time

susan—

food and wine so good. so beautiful here.

the wheel of fortune and rum and cokes—ouch
the memories—remember how you would wait until
she was passed out and meet me down the block?
ttyl, marion

Subject: meeting down the block

Date: 9/6/2007 8:32:32 AM Eastern Standard Time

Sent from: Ssturtz@aol.com

To: Mardor@conde.org

Marion,

We were bad and she never let me forget it, especially not the Grand Finale. Who throws
their pregnant 16-year-old out on the street?
I'm not sure what was worse—being forced to
live with Len and his parents or being abandoned by my mother. It's strange, but when I
think about this, I feel defeated with Amanda.
Maybe I connect my "mistake" with her making
one. Or maybe our fighting reminds me of
fighting with my mom. Amanda is always causing
me such angst, such grief. Last night I tried
giving her a pep talk, but instead it turned
into an all-out brawl over grades. I just want
her to get into a decent school. I just can't

seem to connect with her. I think she's probably hurt that I didn't come after her when she
bled through her bathing suit. The vacation
and bat mitzvah haven't exactly engendered
warm feelings between us. It's hard to let it
all go.

~S

Subject: RE: meeting down the block
Date: 9/7/2007 6:38:52 PM Eastern Standard Time
susan—
you're doing the best you can.
you didn't get a blueprint.
sorry have to scoot.

~m

Subject: a little enlightenment
Date: 9/9/2007 7:40:12 PM Eastern Standard Time
Sent from: Mardor@conde.org
To: Ssturtz@aol.com
susan—
thinking about you. met this spiritual woman
last night, a shaman actually, at this conde
vietnam function.
we were talking about mothers and daughters
(told her about you and girls). ning (the
shaman) told me a story of these mothers and infants during the holocaust—some mothers with

their infants were forced to ride like cattle in the backs of stifling trucks. the mothers held their newborns for hours and no one gave them food or water. the first thump was heard . . . and then another thump came. thump . . . thump . . . thump . . . until there were no sounds. so awful. the mothers did not have the strength to hold on, to give to their babies, ning said.

then she said this—if there is nothing given, there is nothing to give.

i thought of your mother . . . and how she was abused and how her dad abandoned them.

you are not your mother. you've already broken the cycle.

remember how you felt when you found out you were going to have a girl? you said you'd never be able to have a mother-daughter relationship. now you have two. maybe not perfect every day. but . . . what is?

miss you. love you, marion

14

> The first step to better times
> is to imagine them.

When school began, I swore it would be different. And not in the ways The Captain cared about. Entering the cold halls of the high school, with its traces of perfume and newly painted walls, I felt like it was a new start. New haircut, new makeup, cute first-day outfit—I told myself I was a new Amanda. And absolutely *nothing* like Himmel*fart*! Things were going to get better for me; maybe not at home, but definitely in school. Fakey Flakey was going to wish—no, *dream*—*she* could be *me*. I'd stay close to Paige, of course, and chill with my other friends, but I was going to have a hot boyfriend and be seen as a popular girl—be accepted, wanted somewhere.

A week into school Paige and I fell into a daily routine. We'd meet at the same place every day and walk to our first-period classes together. I was glad summer was over—even if swim practices were tough and homework was already piling up.

One morning Paige was waiting for me, leaning against a wall, totally immersed in a book. She was wearing her all-too-familiar leather coat. She wears it like it's part of her personality. Hot or cold, rain or shine, the leather is on.

"Hey," I said.

"Omigod. Your hair looks so hot," she said.

"Thanks. You look cute too, even with that old rag," I joked, pointing to her leather coat. Sometimes the thing on my mind I know I shouldn't say is exactly what I do say.

"What's wrong with this?" she asked, grabbing one side of the coat and slapping her other hand on her hip.

"Nothing. It's just you never take it off."

"I'm wearing it for as long as it fits. Thank God it was huge when I first got it. Now it fits perfectly. I love it. It gives me this feeling . . . I don't know . . . it's hard to explain."

"Okay. You're weird."

"It's like a bubble around me, shielding me from the world, like it protects me."

"Wow," I said, making some spooky sounds, stirring the air around her. "That's some special, powerful coat you've got there."

"Yeah . . . it is, Amanda." She wrapped it closer around her. Before Paige continued, I knew I had misread what she was saying. I got that uncomfortable feeling you get when you know you've said the wrong thing. "My dad gave it to me, you know, before. . . . Y'know what he told me when he gave it to me?"

"What?"

" 'Carry it well and it'll carry you.' "

I didn't know what to say.

"It was as if he knew what was going to happen," she added, trailing off into her own world. That was something else we both did—take off suddenly to a faraway place. The subject of her dad, anybody's dad, often caused her to space out.

"I'm sorry. You never told me. . . . I didn't know it was from him, and I'm not saying I don't like it, 'cause I really do. I swear I do," I promised softly, wishing I'd kept my fat trap shut.

When I thought about what her dad said—*Carry it well and it'll carry you*—I wished the jacket were mine. I was jealous of it, her dad's message and Paige's faith in all of it. I felt really guilty for feeling this way, especially since my dad was still around.

And what Paige's dad said reminded me of something mine had said to me on the day of my bat mitzvah. *Know yourself and then others can know you.* It had stuck in my head, probably because he didn't often say serious stuff. I didn't have a jacket or anything to wear to remind me of what our dads were saying, but I knew it would be smarter to keep those words in mind instead of caring about what everyone else thinks. It bothered me that wanting to reinvent myself weighed this wisdom out, but the truth is, it did.

Secure Leather
Does that leather jacket
Carry security, confidence and a helping hand?
Does it throw off
Not only heat, like a blast furnace, but strength too?
Will to keep going and an ease?
Does that leather jacket
Bring you the ability to know exactly what to say
To a desperate friend who needs to be loved?
Can I try that leather jacket on someday?
Or will it only work for you?

9.11.07 by A.S.H.

Like an idiot, the following day I said, "Nice coat. I really do like it. Seriously."

"Thanks, glad my friend the fashion police approves."

I wanted to do a better job of fixing my comment about the coat, but Deanna and Brooke came rushing up to us, and we all did a foursome hug and began talking a mile a minute at the same time, the way we do. I felt a bit out of the loop when they talked more about their summers, even though they said they had missed me.

I told them about how the last few weeks of my summer

had sucked. "I was pretty much chained to my bedpost. Two weeks with no Internet was like prison—thank God my dad snuck the laptop to me now and then." I ignored Deanna's remark about how being chained up sounded interesting. She's such a nympho.

"Never mind your prison sentence. We still haven't heard about the good stuff—about Paul," Deanna pressed, snapping her gum and twirling her black flat-ironed hair with her forefinger.

"Never you mind," I teased. I wasn't in any mood to share that Paul had blocked me from his friends list, especially not with Deanna.

"Oh, come on. What happened when you saw him?" Brooke asked eagerly. She had it so easy. Since sixth grade boys had been interested in her. She acted like it was no big deal having so many boys have crushes on her. That would be a big deal to me.

"Stuff. I already told you that we just made out." I threw Paige a *when are they going to stop questioning me about him* look.

Deanna kept her eyes on mine and spiraled her finger out of her hair. She placed her hand over her mouth and gasped. "A-manda. You did it. You did more than make out. You hooked up."

I gave Paige a look.

"Shut up, Deanna," Paige said. "She doesn't feel like talking about it."

"Is that why you got grounded?" asked Brooke. "Did you hook up with him?"

"You *have* to tell us—I always tell you everything," Deanna said, grabbing me by the arms and looking at me all wild-eyed. I wanted to tell her that she told me everything because she was proud of her record, and that I wasn't so sure I wanted a rep like hers. I just wanted a boyfriend. But I didn't want to be in a fight with her. Fighting was a thing I'd had more than my fair share of. Besides, Deanna wasn't about to give in. I'd have to give her the juice at some point.

"It's not like I went all the way or anything."

"Oh, you didn't go all the way, but you did something else . . . hmmm?" She giggled.

Brooke jumped in. "You didn't answer me. Is he the reason you were grounded?"

"Yeah, that's why. I snuck out with him and got into a huge war with my mom. Remember the night she picked me up in White Plains?"

Deanna laughed. "You called that one *Beat Me on the Street,* right?"

"Sheesh, who could forget that? I thought the cab driver was gonna lay her out." Paige laughed, trying to make light of the memory. I could tell she was trying to shift the focus of our conversation away from Paul. It was one of those times I remember thinking that she was a better friend to me than I was to her.

"Your mom is, like, on crack," Deanna blurted.

"Deanna. Harsh," Brooke said. Just then, Tommy, Brooke's boyfriend, came up behind her. She turned around to face him, all happy. He gave her a quick kiss and said, "Meet me at my locker."

Paige was basically telling Deanna off. "Would you like me to say a few things about your mom?" she asked her.

"You'd better not," Deanna warned.

I stepped next to Paige and glared at Deanna. "Exactly the point. You shouldn't talk."

"Come on, you guys. Don't fight," Brooke pleaded, back in the conversation. With her, everything should always be perfect and pretty. *Live my life a day*, I'd wanted to tell her on several occasions.

"Sorry, Amanda, I shouldn't be all in your business about your mom. I just thought we were close enough for you to talk to me," Deanna said.

A loud bell rang, signaling us to get to homeroom.

"Saved by the bell," Deanna said. "You can fill us in at lunch . . . if you want to, that is," she said. She gave me her fake smile.

"Yeah, and wait for me to get there before you say one word?" Brooke said, rushing to meet Tommy.

"Okay, okay," I said, partly glad to have my info in such high demand and partly annoyed that Deanna was making such a big deal about me and Paul. Like she almost couldn't believe I, *Amanda*, had hooked up with someone. "Sometimes I wonder why we're friends with her," I complained to Paige.

"I guess because we've been friends for so long." Paige was rummaging through her backpack. "Where is that damn thing?"

"What are you looking for?" I asked.

"Here it is." She pulled a gift out.

"What's this for?" I took it and ripped off the wrapping paper. It was *The Book Thief*. "I've been dying to read this."

"It's really from my mom. She bought it for me too so we can read it at the same time."

"Your mom is the best."

Sometimes it hurt to watch Paige and her mom, especially seeing them kiss and hug all the time.

15

Untried Days

Seasons come and pass,
Plants swish and sway,
I stand,
Just waiting,
For wind's ballet.
I twist and tangle,
In the mystery
I ask myself,
When?
When is it time
I go into Earth's play?
I think,
Think about it,

Every day,
Looking in the mirror,
I say,
Today—today is the day.

9.25.07 by A.S.H.

Every morning when we walked by the rows of rusted red lockers, this one group of guys would make comments about Paige. Before school started she had gotten a new eyebrow piercing. I was surprised when I first saw it. She had said the little hoop was barely noticeable—but you could barely *not* notice it. In my house, tattoos and body piercings were statements of "low class and promiscuity," which my mother boiled down to a life sentence of a slut going nowhere. But she had no idea who Paige was, just like she had no idea who I was.

As we passed the guys, one idiot yelled out, "Nice stockings, Madonna. Don't you know it's not the eighties anymore?"

Embarrassed, I looked down, but not Paige. She looked right through them and continued to talk to me as if they didn't exist. I loved that she could do that, even though I felt awkward about what she wore. I had to agree with the guys—I didn't get her style, but unlike them, I got *her*. I wished I were her. She was a lot more together than I was.

Embarrassment came easily to me. Take swim practice. And Courtney Flakey. She'd take any opportunity to embarrass me. Then there was Coach Walfish, who'd make an idiot out of you for being late to practice, something I inevitably was. I couldn't help it. Our practices had gotten switched from the usual place to Courtney's mom's fitness club because the roof in the veterans' club where we normally swam was collapsing and under repair.

On one of the first practices, Coach had screamed from across the pool, "Amanda Himmelfarb!"

"Yeah?" I mumbled.

Courtney was standing with a group of girls from the team. She didn't even try to hide her snotty giggle. "Himmel*fart is* late—twenty laps," she laughed, flipping her blond hair over to the side. Paige was so right about all of Courtney's friends—they were despicable loser wannabes sucking up to Miss Asshole Queen Bee herself.

"Courtney," Coach said in a halfhearted reprimanding voice. "Amanda, you know the drill. Twenty laps."

It was times like these that I needed Paige by my side so that I could tell Fakey Flakey and her friends off. I called The Cap from a pay phone and told her I was staying to talk to the coach after practice and did my extra twenty laps then. Afterward, I got out of the pool and quickly showered, leaving the locker room with a wet head to avoid the rest of the team.

That was the afternoon I first talked to Rick Hayes. I knew who he was—everyone knew who he was.

"Do you have change for a dollar?" he asked me as he held up a crinkly bill. Rick was one of the hottest guys at Stone Creek High *and* Courtney's boyfriend.

"I—I think so," I stammered, sifting through my gym bag. I could feel my stomach bubbling, gurgling. *Please don't fart. Please don't fart.* I pulled out change, a nickel short of a dollar. "Sorry, I only have ninety-five cents," I said, holding my palm out to him and squeezing my butt cheeks tighter.

"Here," he said, handing the bill to me. "You can owe me. Hey, you're in tenth, right?" he asked, loading coins into the snack machine.

"Um . . . yeah . . . I am."

He reached down and grabbed his Skittles. "Want some?"

"No thanks."

"Okay. See you around." He lifted his chin to me and walked away. Courtney came out of the locker room a second later, and they walked off together arm in arm. I thought when he looked back he winked at me, but I wasn't positive. I was in a trance because he'd spoken to me.

When I told Paige, Brooke and Deanna the following day, everyone except Paige got excited for me. She really couldn't have cared less. Rick and C.K. were exactly the kind of guys Paige despised. In her mind, *she* was too cool for *them*.

"Omigod. He's so hot. I totally want his friend Casey Kahn," Deanna said.

"Those boys are so immature," Paige said.

"Rick's nice. He's not like C. K." I was already defending him, even though I knew nothing about him. But neither did Paige.

"He's another child." She shrugged.

"You always say don't judge a book by its cover. You don't know him."

"Whatever," she said.

"And the cover"—I shook my head—"is not shabby. He's serious eye candy, is what he is: tall, dirty-blond with a great build, and melt-your-insides killer green eyes."

We searched for a spot in the commons toward the back wall.

The front was where the gay and lesbian groups, the ultimate Frisbee players and the Hacky Sack guys gathered. The back of the commons was the main area in the high school where more groups hung out: the preps, Goths, nerds, stoners, boarders, jocks, punks, etc. A redheaded kid with khaki pants and a white T-shirt walked in, and we made predictions about which group he would sit with.

I had held off on telling "the Paul details" to Brooke and Deanna. I kept going back and forth about whether I wanted to. Paige, of course, knew it already—how I'd given him head and he basically couldn't have cared less if I'd disappeared off the face of the earth. But The Cap's saying Paul only wanted my body and not me I kept to myself. After Brooke and Deanna begged again, I finally gave in and began with Paul and me holding hands and walking to the lifeguard chair, which in many ways was the best part. There were lots of "omigods" and "keep goings" as I spoke.

Deanna said, "Even if you just blew him, you're no virgin anymore."

"Yes, she is," Paige said. "Giving a guy head doesn't mean you lose your virginity."

"Who are you to say?" Deanna asked her.

"They didn't have sex," Paige said.

"Yeah, maybe if you're going by the definition your grandparents had."

"So it's a matter of opinion, but your opinion is in the minority."

"She's a virgin if she didn't do it," Brooke said, facing Deanna. "You know damn well it's different."

"Maybe. Going down is more personal, if you ask me," Deanna said.

I didn't bother defending my virginity to Deanna; I just shoveled out the rest of the details. *I might as well*, I figured, unraveling the story in a matter-of-fact tone. A weird thing happened. I began not to recognize my own voice: Suddenly I felt stunned by what I was saying—stunned by *my own mouth*.

16

The days you swim
are days you can drown.

Swim team had the first of the mandatory evening meetings
that Coach Walfish liked to pull on us. Coach wanted to
set us up with which events we would swim. I wanted the
butterflyers' #1 spot in the medley relay, but I knew that
Courtney also wanted it, and her time was always a second
or two less than mine. It wouldn't hurt that we were using
Courtney's club. *Favors go far*, I thought. It was nauseating
listening to Coach overdo the thanks to Fakey Flakey. "Let's
hear it for Courtney for supplying this pool." The team
cheered.

"Okay," Coach said, "so we lost two seniors last year, two
important seniors who could fly." She scanned the team.
"Remember we were number one in states last year."

"Don't worry, Coach, I can fly," Courtney said, leaning

up against Brittany, our team captain. Some of these girls would let her step on their faces if she wanted to.

"I'll fly, if you want me to," I offered with one hundred degrees less confidence than Fakey Flakey.

"You go, Court," Brittany said, giving her a playful shove.

"We're a team," Coach said to no one in particular. "Amanda, you'll make an excellent alternate for the top medley team, but Courtney, we'll start you with the first spot this year."

The team cheered for both of us but I knew it was more for Courtney.

Coach Walfish moved on to the keep-your-grades-up, self-discipline speech. When we looked sufficiently bored the way high school students mostly look in first period, practically asleep, she let us go.

While waiting for my mother to pick me up, I saw Rick Hayes again. He got out of an Audi and leaned against it. *He's so incredibly hot,* I thought as our eyes met. My heart stopped. My knees nearly buckled. It was a crazy, paralyzing, dizzying second that broke like heavy glass thrown out of a tenth-story window when Courtney came crashing out of the building. I realized that she must have sensed something, or she caught him looking in my direction. She put a hand on her hip and flashed an evil grin at me before taking all his attention away. She looked back at me, and I waited for her to say it, to destroy what he maybe saw in me.

"Hey, Court," I could hear Rick say, pushing himself off

the car. He grabbed her and kissed her. She said something in his ear and then giggled, staring my way. Rick never looked back at me. They got into his car and drove away. I figured that the next time I saw Rick Hayes, he'd think, *Himmelfart*.

17

I didn't talk to Rick again until a couple days later after school, at the 24-7 deli. Paige and I had decided to walk there and split a sandwich.

Rick was in line ordering. "Can I have a turkey and roast beef combo on a wedge? Shredded lettuce, tomato and Russian dressing too, please." I loved the sound of his gravelly voice.

I stood back, looking at the menu board, pretending I didn't see him.

He noticed me and then, out of the corner of my eye, I watched him make his way to where Paige and I were standing.

"Hey," he said. My stomach flipped.

"Hi."

"You got a nickel?"

"Huh? Oh . . . ummm . . . yeah. . . ." I started to rummage through my purse.

"I'm just kiddin'," he laughed, patting me on the shoulder. "Remember you gave me change for a dollar?" All I could think about was how cute his hair looked and his adorable green eyes. And his full lips.

"Oh yeah," I said, pretending I didn't remember, though I'd only replayed it in my head a ridiculous number of times.

"You wanna go order?" Paige interrupted.

"Okay—one sec." I nodded, turning my full attention back to Rick.

"So, you're a swimmer too?" he asked.

"Yeah." I forced myself to sound cool, like no big deal. I remembered Courtney's grin when Rick had picked her up from the swim meeting—she thought she was so much better than I was. I hated her even more for making me think she was right. I vowed to myself I would do whatever it took to leave behind the shadow of unpopular Amanda Himmelfarb. The fact that Rick seemed to be flirting a little with me was the icing on the cake. *Talk about perfect in-your-face*, I thought—stealing the boyfriend from the creator of the Himmel*fart* legacy.

"Amanda, I'm on the line," Paige called to me.

"You pick. I'll go for anything." She raised her eyebrows at me in a way that said, *Yeah, I can see*.

"So, do you come here every day after school?" he asked, sticking a hand in his pocket and pulling out change. As he counted, I answered, steadying my hands and managing my stomach.

"Pretty much," I lied. I was glad that Paige was ordering and couldn't hear.

Before practice I was supposed to report directly to the library, something I never did but lied about all the time. This way The Cap couldn't reach me on my cell to check up on me. Aunt Jen teased her about being a New Age helicopter parent—always hovering.

"Want a ride tomorrow? I know it's lazy, but I usually drive down to make a quick pit stop here before football practice." He handed money to the cashier and grabbed his sandwich.

"Sure. Um, but won't Courtney throw a fit? We're not the best of friends, you know."

"Yeah, I know. But look." He held up his arms. "No chains." He chuckled. "So?"

"Okay. Sure." I could not believe this was true. That Rick Hayes might be interested in me and that I could actually steal Courtney's boyfriend. I imagined the look on her face. I could just imagine the look on a lot of people's faces.

18

You think it's a secret, but it has
never been one.

After that time at the deli, I started meeting Rick every day. The more I saw him, the further my grades dropped. I was supposed to do homework between school and swim practice, but I had been going off with Rick instead and making out with him in his car parked in the back of the senior parking lot. For the first few times, we *only* made out. And then we started skipping the deli to fool around even more, though we told each other we just weren't hungry. *We were plenty hungry, just not for food.*

I let him go under my shirt and touch me over my pants, and I had touched him outside his jeans. I don't know how he dealt with changing into gym clothes for practice—I left ready to jump in the pool with my clothes on.

Our routine was pretty much all I could think about—

that and the look on Fakey Flakey's face when she found out we were together. Courtney still had no idea. According to Rick, her mother had her come straight to the club every day after school. Rick kept saying he was going to break up with her any day. He was just trying to figure out how to do it in a nice way.

"She's gonna figure it out," I told him.

He said, "Only C.K. knows, and he's my boy. He won't say anything." I reassured him it wouldn't get out from my end before he told Courtney himself.

The other thing I couldn't stop thinking about was the homecoming dance. He hadn't mentioned the dance, and every time I planned to, it seemed like the wrong moment. I had told Aunt Jen a little about Rick, and she said, "Go for what you want, Amanda. You be in control." Rick was what I wanted, so finally I brought it up.

"Did you do it? Break up with her?" I asked him the next day when we were together.

"Technically, I'm already sort of broken up with her. I mean, I'm with you, y'know, more."

"It's not the same as her knowing."

"She's not fun like you." He was rubbing my leg and playing with my belt.

"If she's no fun, why are you *technically* with her?" I pushed his hands away.

"I swear that I'm going to break it off with her. I'm just waiting for the right time."

"Still?"

"Two nights ago I tried to, but she cried and told her mom. Then her mom saw my mom at the market, and my mom forced me to call Courtney so that we could talk and figure stuff out."

"What does that mean? What did she say?"

"Who?"

"Courtney. Your mom. You're, like, giving me half the story."

"I told her I'd meet up with her later and we'd talk."

"And she left it at that?"

"She thinks we're still together. I'm doing the best I can. Why are you giving me such a hard time?"

"Let me get my violin," I said. I swatted his hand away again. "I want you to break up, already."

"All right, all right," he promised, grabbing my belt again, pressing himself against me as much as he could, given the stick shift. This time I let him, hoping that it would persuade him to finish Courtney off. I wanted him to think that's what he'd have to do if he wanted *me* to *finish him off*.

But it didn't work. Another week went by and they were still *technically* together. I even caught him in the hall hugging her. He said he was consoling her, telling her how they could still be friends. Though I figured he was lying, for some reason I fooled myself into believing it was at least half true.

The word around school was that they'd had a lover's quarrel. Paige kept reporting Rick sightings. "I saw Slick Rick with Fakey Flakey," or "I saw that loser, Rick, with his bigger loser sidekick, C.K."

Finally, I snapped. "Not everyone can live up to your standards."

"What's that supposed to mean?" she asked.

"You know, how you expect everyone to be a certain way."

"I don't expect anyone to be anyone they're not. Just like I don't think you should try to be someone you're not."

"So now I'm a poseur because I like a hot guy who likes me?"

"You're the one who knows the answer to that."

"I do?" I said angrily.

"Yeah, you do." She picked up her backpack and walked away.

Later that night I called her. She apologized before I could even get the words out.

"Maybe we shouldn't bring Rick up in our conversations anymore," I said.

"I hate that you can't talk to me about him. But—"

"I never want a guy to come between us," I said.

"Neither do I—they're so not worth it."

"I like him, though, and just don't want to hear shit about him—you know?"

"Yeah. I know," she said. We talked about other unimportant things, like homework and who Deanna was with that week, and then we hung up. That was the last time she asked about Rick. It was like she had given up on me. It reminded me a little of how The Cap made me feel. But it didn't stop how much I wanted Rick. In fact, it kind of made me want him even more.

19

A conclusion is simply the place
where you got tired of thinking.

One afternoon in Rick's car we started this little game. "How bad do you want me to break up with Courtney?" he'd ask. I'd answer with a hot kiss. "*This* bad." Then he'd say, "Wait, how bad?" and I'd press myself a little closer and say, "*This* bad." We repeated this a couple times until finally he said, "Okay, *whoa.* You're driving me so crazy. I can't take it anymore. I'm gonna break up with Court and tell her—"

My stomach sank like a rock when he said his little nickname for her. *He's still into her; it's Court, not Courtney.*

"I don't believe you'll do it," I said.

He was like, "C'mon, I'll even go to the next swim meet and cheer for you. That'll prove it. But let me be with you . . . y'know, *that* way, because I want to be with you *this* bad." He put my hand over his zipper. He felt like concrete!

"Oh . . . *that* way!" I answered playfully, although with Paul and the lifeguard chair in my head, I pulled my hand away. "I'm not as experienced as you might think."

"Really? You seem like you are."

My first thought was, *Use it to your advantage*.

"I don't know," I teased, lightly brushing his lips.

"I want you sooo bad," he said, grabbing my hand and putting it back on his hardness, trying to move me toward him.

"Ummm, yeah . . ."

"So? Show me?" He pouted, all adorable.

I looked around the parking lot. "No. Not *here*."

"How about I take you out and then you can do it?" he said, pulling me closer. "So hot," he whispered.

"Where?" I asked, giving him little feathery wet kisses. I wanted him to take me out. "When?" I wanted him to choose me. *Choose me, choose me*—my lips pressed into his. I wanted him to want me more than Courtney—enough to be his girlfriend. Enough to share secrets. Enough to care about each other. My tongue played tag with his, and I used it to transmit my message: *You just may get what you want if you choose me*.

"Whenever you want," he said, breathing heavier.

"What about homecoming?" I made an *o* with my lips around his tongue. "That's the whenever for the whatever." The gold medal within my reach. *Take control like Aunt Jen said*.

"I don't know. I'm, like, supposed to bring Courtney. I asked her months ago, you know."

The mention of her name made me feel like bursting into tears.

"Oh," I said, crushed. I pulled away from him. "Then take her . . . and . . . you can have her do that. I gotta get to practice." I opened the car door to get out.

"Come on, don't be like that," he said, pulling me back. "When you say 'for the whatever,' how far do you mean?" He pulled me toward him and kissed me softly on my neck. He was so hard to resist. I wanted him so badly.

"I don't know." *Choose me*, I kissed back. I willed his mind with my tongue to say, *You're it*.

"Tell me *all the way*, is all I'm saying." He slid his hand in between my crossed legs. I tightened around them.

My mind worked toward its mission: *become Rick Hayes's girlfriend, beat Courtney, become somebody*. "You know what you just asked for," I said, pulling his hand away. "I'll give you that." I felt weirdly guilty, like I was offering to commit a crime.

"I'll tell you what." He paused. "I'll make a deal with you. If you promise *everything*, then I promise to take you to the dance. And I'll pay. We'll go like we're really *together*. Y'know, like a couple." He was saying all the right things, as if he could read my mind. The Captain had a way of doing this too—the reading my mind part.

"Um, I don't know. *It* should be special," I said, thinking that I didn't want to say *I'm a virgin* but if I was going to do it, I wanted to look gorgeous and dance slow with him and make sure my first time would be the best night ever.

"It'll be special." He kissed me and smoothed my hair.

"What a sport you are, offering to buy the tickets," I teased, trying to think. Being a couple for the dance but not yet officially a couple in school bothered me. But afterward we'd be a couple, so long as *it* was good, I guessed. I continued to rework The Deal in my head, turning it over and over—I wanted him to be with me, not Courtney. I wanted to be his girlfriend. I wanted everyone to see us in the halls, holding hands and kissing.

"I'm a sport and your date to homecoming . . . if you want."

If I want?

Then he brought me closer to him and said, "Tell me tomorrow what you want to do." I rested my forehead on his chin and he kissed it. It was one of those moments. The ones that you know will just stay with you forever. He pulled my chin up so that our lips met, then kissed me with kisses lighter than air. I was speechless.

"I'll bring money for the tickets so I'm set on my end of the deal, okay, Manda?"

That was it. The *Manda* sealed it.

Once in a while a blue moon would hang from the sky and my mother would be a mom. She'd say, "Manda, do you need something?" when I'd get the bad chlorine burn behind my eyes that would turn into a migraine. She'd bring me up some hot tea and aspirin, the way she'd do for Aunt Jen sometimes. I locked each scene, each time in my mind—me curled up in my bed under a warm blanket, her long, pretty fingers dunking the tea bag a few more times, wrapping it around the spoon and squeezing every ounce of flavor into the cup. It was a big contrast to the usual Suffer In Silence treatment. Usually, it was more like, *Enough, Amanda. Turn your lights off if your eyes hurt, Amanda. Get some sleep and you'll be fine, Amanda.* Or my favorite, *There's nothing I can do for you, Amanda.* Rare as it was, the sound of *Manda* automatically made me feel a bit better.

Clearly I needed to get my head examined, because even though his "Okay, Manda" was at least partly about me agreeing to sleep with him, I still heard myself say, "Set on my end too. It's a deal."

20

> The skills you have gathered
> will one day come in handy.

Before Paul, I felt like a loser. So climbing up the lifeguard chair—ladder of lust—with him seemed reasonable enough. But going *all the way* with Rick was hard to justify, even when *being with him* was the one good thing in my life. I still wasn't so sure about allowing something that was twice the width (or more) of a tampon inside me. Deanna had said, "It's *nothing* like a tampon— much bigger. The first time was like getting cut open." I might have been raised to SIS, Suffer In Silence, but no one has a lower pain threshold—I feel pain just thinking about pain. Aunt Jen had told me she's the same way and that the way people experience pain is closely tied to their sense of empathy and compassion. This explained The Captain's high tolerance for it.

I secretly knew I'd made myself feel good imagining how *it* would feel. But imagination was something I controlled.

Pain and bliss were opposite, and I realized I could wind up anywhere on the spectrum.

I really wasn't sure if I wanted to take that leap with anyone yet. It haunted me that I had made a deal to go all the way with Rick in return for a date to *a dance*. Plus, if something went wrong, I could end up pregnant. I doubted this would happen, but it crossed my mind anyway. What if the apple didn't fall far from the tree? Even if just a little, I worried some curse was on my family. I tried to push it out of my head and not think about what my mother would do if she found out I'd traded my virginity for a dance. My head swam until I wasn't sure of anything anymore, except that when I was with Rick I didn't feel like a loser. So I agreed to The Deal. I told no one—kept it a secret, afraid that if I tried to justify my reasoning, it wouldn't stand up to a tiny breeze. At least I had made Rick promise that he'd break it off with Courtney by the end of the week. We were so close yet also scary far from being a couple, the thing I wanted more than anything. In the back of my mind, I worried Courtney would change Rick's mind, and then she'd be going to the homecoming dance and I'd be Amanda Himmel*fart*, alone at home.

I couldn't ask Paige for advice, so I turned to Aunt Jen. She had some great ideas how to get The Cap's permission to go to the dance and get the dress I wanted. I told myself everything would work out the way I wanted. Aunt Jen said, "Permission first. Dress second." She promised, "I'll help you cross that bridge when you get to it."

Her bridge comment made me think of the winter vacation

when my family crossed the border into Jordan from Israel. The Captain was like the border policeman who interrogated us. If the dance was Jordan, The Captain was border patrol. I'd have to get my papers in order—my story straight—to get past the checkpoint. Those first weeks of sophomore year, we settled into a state of relaxed tension—a détente, she called it— and I dreaded disturbing it, but I needed her permission.

"You should frame it as a group date. You're not *really* lying, because you'll be with your friends," Aunt Jen said.

"Yeah, true."

"Your strategy should include a good attitude before you ask. You know how your mouth gets you into trouble," she reminded me.

She was right; I'd have to remember The Captain's powerful antennae: I needed to be careful, say the right things and not let my body speak a different language. Like when answering the Jordanian border policeman's questions, I'd have to keep my answers tight, devoid of suspicious interpretations, and my mannerisms consistent with my story. My mantra would be no attitude, no body language and especially no hand on my hip, which makes The Captain crazy.

The right moment came when I found her in the kitchen preparing dinner. I told myself to be calm and casual, and to keep my sarcasm under control. Then I went for the green light.

"The first home football game is coming up," I announced. I paused to give her a chance to respond. She was chopping cucumbers.

She stopped what she was doing and looked up at me. "So?"

"Well . . . there's also the homecoming dance," I said. She went back to slicing.

"And?"

"Which is sort of not as important as the game, because it's the game that everyone is—" I was trying to make the dance seem like an afterthought, but before I could finish, her antennae rose.

"Who's going to the dance?" The Captain was now roughly peeling the skin off a red onion.

"Everyone," I answered.

"It's mostly an upperclassmen scene, isn't it? I heard there was a problem with drinking last year." She threw the peels in the trash and began slicing.

"If it's a bad situation, I'll call. We just care about hanging out together. And the dancing."

She didn't say anything. She just wiped her eye and continued slicing.

"We're going as a group," I offered.

"Who's in the group?"

"Brooke and the usual crew," I said. Brooke was who I always used for my alibis because she was the only one of my friends The Captain approved of. She was the type parents like: superpolite, nicely dressed, in all AP classes. Always poured on the manners. "Hi, Mrs. Himmelfarb." "You look so nice, Mrs. Himmelfarb."

"I assume Paige and Deanna are part of this group?"

"I don't know. Probably. I think so." Her tone and being

114

interrogated dug through me but I couldn't show it. Not if I wanted to go to the dance with Rick.

"I'm going with Brooke, but everyone will be there."

Her eyes ran their usual inspection, up and down.

"What time is it supposed to end?" She crinkled her brow.

"Elevenish."

"Okay, and who's driving and picking up?"

"Brooke's father is taking us and picking us up cuz she wants me to sleep at her house afterward."

"*Be*-cause."

"Right. If that's okay?"

"I'd rather you sleep here. Brooke can come here."

"Okay. Brooke's dad could pick us up." I hadn't asked Brooke yet, but I'd beg her so I wouldn't have to worry about an embarrassing scene. Under the circumstances, The Captain was too unpredictable to be allowed near the school.

"So you're going with your group. Is that your story?" Her eyes were watering from the onion and she dabbed at them with a paper towel.

My story? It annoyed me that she assumed I was stretching the truth. Even if I was.

"Call Brooke's house if you don't believe me."

"I don't need your permission to call, but it's a good idea."

Then, of course, came the rules: Rules #505, #506 and #517.

"Obviously, no drinking. Certainly, no smoking. I don't want you doing anything that there's a one in a million chance I wouldn't approve of. That's what you should use as your barometer if reason and values elude you. I don't want another Myrtle Beach."

As I watched her mouth, I imagined her surgically implanting a GPS chip inside me to track my location at all times.

She went on and on, and I thought, *Why can't she just be clueless like my friends' parents? Paige's mother—she's her friend; Brooke's—all that matters is Brooke's happiness; Deanna's—can't deal with her; my mother—up my ass!*

"Do you hear me?" she asked.

"I hear you." *You don't trust me.*

After all that, she said she still needed to talk to my dad about it. This was ridiculous since we both knew she made the decisions. It was a buy-time trick. Anyway, I felt unusually optimistic because she threatened to ground me from every future social activity if I did anything I shouldn't be doing, or if I forgot to call her if any plans changed. The calling thing I took seriously since *Beat Me on the Street,* where she'd smacked me in front of my friends. I didn't call when I had gone to a late movie in White Plains with Paige, Brooke and Deanna and had missed the train home. It had been nothing short of woman-to-woman combat.

21

> The great pleasure in life is doing
> what people say you cannot do.

Later that night my parents came into my room to "discuss" the dance. They stood above me, dominating and powerful, seemingly together, but I knew better. The way they'd been fighting, it was like we were living in a house of cards. Ganging up on me was a way for them to make peace with each other.

"We're going to give you a clean slate, Amanda. But we want you to make better decisions. You're like a bird that can't stop flying into windows," La-La Man said.

I rolled my eyes to the ceiling.

"It's that kind of attitude that keeps getting you into trouble," he said, shifting his weight.

"I didn't even say anything," I protested, making sure not to roll my eyes *again*.

"Actions speak louder than words. You don't have to say anything."

My body tensed and I struggled to control my attitude, but it took on a voice of its own. "What*ever*."

"You see?" The Captain said, pointing at me and looking at La-La Man.

My dad didn't acknowledge her. "Amanda, don't pull an attitude. *I'm* trying to help you here."

"That's not right!" my mother barked. "What did we just talk about?"

"What?" He looked at her and threw his arms up in the air.

"*That*—'*I'm* trying to help.' You always make yourself the good guy. As if you're the only one who said that she could go."

"Are we here to discuss us or her?" Dad looked at me and said, "You need to be more responsible."

"I will be responsible. I promise."

"I knew this would happen," The Captain fumed.

"Again we're back to *you*," he said.

I watched, but I didn't really hear them. Then from a distance I heard my dad say, "We want to be able to trust you, Amanda."

Blah, blah, blah. I blocked it out. Same speech, new voice—still *bor*-ing and annoying. My mother had stopped arguing with him and was now staring past me, biting her bottom lip, saying nothing.

I stared down at my comforter. There was lint on it. I pulled it away one piece at a time. *She hates me. She hates me not.*

I spoke to my dad.

"I want the chance to prove that you *can* trust me."

"*I* do trust you, Amanda," my father said.

A weird *pfft* sound escaped from the pinhole between my mother's pursed lips.

"I know you want to do the right thing," he continued. I nodded.

"It's just that when you've been burned so many times, you don't want to go back to the fire. Do you know what I mean?" he asked.

"Yes. I'll stay away from the fire," I promised.

"No. I mean, *you're* the fire and *we've* been burned." He glanced at my mother, then back at me. "By you."

"Oh." My cheeks burned.

"Amanda." My mother cleared her throat. "This will be your last chance. No more lies and manipulation."

My father shifted and mumbled something under his breath.

"Did you say something?" She spun around.

"I said, 'It's getting late and we should let her get to bed.' "

She looked at me. "Don't repeat your mistakes. You're making it harder on yourself and everyone else in this house."

"Yes. I know. I'm the one who causes all the problems," I said.

"That's not the route you want to take here, trust me."

"Sorry," I mumbled, completely not. "God, it's just a dance. It's not like I'm asking for permission to go clubbing in the city."

"It always amazes me how flippant you get when you're the one who sets these situations in motion, especially considering *you* want something."

Hearing the anger rising in her voice, I started to panic. *Focus on the dance. What are you doing here, getting her all pissed off?* A golden window of opportunity had opened and I was about to slam it shut.

"I'm sorry. I promise I won't screw up." I remembered to speak with respect.

Before she left my room, The Captain paused a moment, and I braced myself. Then she just left. I pulled at the lint some more. *She hates me. She hates me not.*

Petals off a Flower
Petals off a flower
The smile outta my step
I wear weariness as a necklace
For I am tired of having to pray.
Victimized by being the only one
In a single-handed band
I play my own music
Sing my own songs
I can't play a duet here
Nor can I play a simple melody

All the music I make is a repetitive beat
I can't change it now
The beat has become habit
Taking on its own life form
The beat looks like what I see in the mirror
I am ongoing
I am going nowhere
Still a flower
with every petal picked off.

10.9.07 by A.S.H.

22

Subject: School Dance and Romance—Yikes!

Date: 10/10/07 7:18:42 PM Eastern Standard Time

Sent from: Ssturtz@aol.com

To: Mardor@conde.org

Marion,

How are you? There's a lot of excitement in the Himmelfarb house. Amanda's going to homecoming. I can't believe she's this age already. Truthfully, I'm afraid of what she'll do. But I'm also happy for her. She seems excited. Len and I laid down some rules here. After all, we all know exactly what can happen.

I miss you.

Love, Susan

Subject: RE: School Dance and Romance—Yikes!

Date: 10/11/07 10:12:54 PM Eastern Standard Time

susan,

tell amanda I'm excited for her.

so busy here. so great tho. seeing wonderful things.

but so many deadlines. i guess they are putting the book together faster than we'd all thought. i look forward to my room and going to sleep some nights.

wish i were there to see homecoming hoopla. send pictures.

love,

marion

23

Be unconventional, even visionary.

Aunt Jen, my secret agent, invited herself to go with us to pick out my homecoming dress—my buffer against the potential *Butting Heads over Threads*.

Melody came too, and the four of us attacked the racks, picking out dresses in my size. In the fitting room I put the dresses my mother had picked on a separate hook. I wanted to try on the dresses I liked first. When I came out with dress numero uno, my mother's eyes widened and she pointed back to the fitting room as if she were a traffic cop.

"It's too low-cut," she said, shaking her head.

Rule #532: no cleavage.

"That's the style," I challenged. "It's less low-cut than my pink sweater."

"I don't like that sweater for that very reason, but it was a gift," she said, glancing at Aunt Jen, the giver.

"I think it's hot," announced Melody. I knew exactly what she was doing. Her compliment would make The Captain think the dress was sexy, and therefore inappropriate.

"It does show a little too much. You don't need to showcase the *girls*," Aunt Jen said.

I threw her a dirty look. *Who invited you?*

"Jennifer, please. That's so tacky. *Must* you use slang for body parts?" my mother asked, forcing a lighthearted voice.

"But everyone wears strapless." I didn't want to cave too easily on the first dress. It had taken me a long time to master the art of negotiating with The Captain. I had to begin the wearing-her-down process by selecting stuff that I knew would offend her sensibilities. This way, the dress we would finally settle on, a dress I could live with, wouldn't look too sexy to her.

"Actually," Mel chimed in, checking herself out in the mirror behind me, "she's right, Mom. Strapless is in. That's what everyone wants to wear."

"I don't care what everyone else wears. *You're* not wearing *that*." She waved her finger up and down. "March in there and try on another one."

It *so* irritated me to be flicked away. I'll never do that to *my* daughter.

When my mother turned her back, I looked at Aunt Jen pleadingly.

She shook her head.

Back into the fitting room I went. The next dress was *too tight*. The next *too short*. The next *too low in the back*. Finally, I put on a long violet organza dress that showed just a beginning of cleavage and a hint of leg. I sashayed out to the mirrors like Goldilocks, happy to find the one that was *just right*.

"Oh, Amanda! That's beautiful on you," Aunt Jen said.

"That's killer," Melody said.

I beamed, turning my body to check out all angles.

"What happened to the dresses I picked out?" my mother asked. A bad sign.

"I haven't gotten to them yet. You don't like this one?" I modeled all sides, full of life.

"Not really. Put your hair up. It's so frizzy, I can't even see the back of the dress."

"What's wrong with it? The dress, not my hair." I really liked it. I wanted it. I thought Rick would love it.

"It's too low-cut. Like your aunt said, we know you have breasts now. You don't need to show them."

Melody giggled.

"What should I do? Duct tape them down?" I knew I was playing with fire, but I couldn't help myself.

Aunt Jen flashed me a look. *Shut your trap, A-SAP!*

I knew she was right, and I couldn't risk another *Brawl at the Mall*, so I quickly added, "I'm just so glad to finally have a figure for a sophisticated dress like this."

"Don't merchandise me, Amanda." The Captain could tell I was trying to sell her. And shopping made her feisty.

"I think it's chic, Susan."

"See? Aunt Jen likes it."

"Of course she does," snipped my mother.

Aunt Jen didn't take the bait. "It's very flattering on her."

"I don't want her wearing something that makes her look so . . . mature," my mother said, tightening her jaw.

"She doesn't look too *mature*. Honestly, you're not going to find anything today that doesn't show a little. I agree it's outrageous when a young girl looks sleazy, but this dress is stylish and long. We'll be here all day if you think that the two of you are going to completely agree on a dress."

The Captain inspected me some more, staring mostly at my chest.

I closed my eyes, desperately trying to transfer my thoughts. *Say yes. Say yes.*

"It's not my first choice either," I said. *Lie, lie to get my pie.*

"Okay, Amanda, as long as you wear a wrap."

I almost hugged The Captain, something I hadn't done in longer than I could remember. "Thank you, thank you, thank you." I bounced sideways back into the fitting room. I felt guilty that I just couldn't do it—couldn't actually hug her. I had grabbed her arms and then felt awkward. But I called "Thank you" to her again. I checked out the dress in the mirror by myself. Leaning down and lifting my boobs up, I enhanced the *girls*. I stuck out my chest, modeling for myself. I imagined Rick seeing me in the dress for the first time. He would be proud that I was his date. Courtney would look like an ugly duckling in comparison. Paige would see Rick and me together and realize that we were meant to be. And Brooke and Deanna and everyone in school would watch us slow dancing to "My Love" by Justin Timberlake.

I'd have stayed in the dress and my daydream longer, but The Captain was waiting. So I threw on my clothes and hurried out, scanning for a register with no line to seal *this* deal.

24

Aunt Jen made plans to take me shopping to get shoes and earrings for the dance. But first I had to prevent another *Fume over the Room*. My mother had told me I'd be going nowhere unless my room was spotless. A typical ultimatum.

While I was showering, The Captain had invaded my fort. She piled laundry on my bed to be put away. My desk was covered with headbands, bracelets, lip gloss and other miscellaneous items. A desk drawer that had a mixture of jewelry and knickknacks had been pulled wide open and had a Post-it note stuck on it that simply read, "Clean." I pulled off the Post-it and reached under my bed to grab the box filled with fortunes and notes that I collect. The notes were mostly ones my mother had put in my lunch bag when was little. I picked one up.

Dear Manda,

Have a nice day.

Mommy

I dropped the "Clean" Post-it in the box and slid it back under the bed.

I returned to my desk. I'd had my messy drawer shut so that no one could see inside it. *If I can find what I want in there, why does it matter?*

I couldn't decide what to put away first. It was overwhelming. I forced myself to focus and started with one side of my desk, which was a mess of folders, papers, stationery, clips and pages from magazines. But I got distracted looking at my mom's old copy of *Are You There God? It's Me, Margaret.* The thick sanitary pad Margaret once had to attach to herself using hooks and a belt had been updated to the peel-and-stick kind in my copy. Girls at one time probably felt as if they had to go into hiding for five to seven days, wearing those bulky pads. It was probably why Grandma Sturtz called them diapers.

I jumped when Aunt Jen knocked on my door.

She smiled. "I understand we need this to be spic-and-span before we take off."

"That's the information I have," I said. I was so glad to see her.

"Aunt Merry Maid at your service," she said, shutting the

door behind her. She pointed to the laundry on my bed and to the dressers and circled her finger in the air, indicating *wrap it up*. "Let's turn this baby around. Chop chop, cadet!"

Shortly after, The Captain came upstairs and gave the go-ahead. Aunt Jen and I rushed and out the door, giggling about the record time it took to clean up my quarters.

25

We had a great time at the mall. Aunt Jen bought me killer open-toed, high-heeled sandals and chandelier earrings. After we finished shopping, we went to my favorite dessert place and ordered pie and mochaccinos.

"Amanda, I see you like to put what you have up there on display," Aunt Jen said, pointing to my boobage.

"You sound like my mother."

"Just saying that shirt's a little low when you lean over."

"Everyone wears these," I said.

"I believe in leaving a little to the imagination."

"The guys I seem to like aren't abstract thinkers; they like the real thing," I laughed.

"You have a lot more to offer than just your body." She didn't find me funny. She sounded serious.

The waiter came over to see if everything was okay, and I noticed him checking Aunt Jen out.

"We're good." She smiled. "Where were we?"

"My cleavage." I laughed again. This time she did too.

"Amanda." She leaned over. "You're still a virgin, right?"

"Aunt Jen. Omigod." I almost choked on my mochaccino.

"Don't be embarrassed. You know you can talk to me."

"I know. But why would you ask that?" I bumbled.

"Because I've got a vibe going. I get the sense that something's up."

"*Yeah*, I am," I whispered, worrying that the table next to us could hear.

"Would you tell me if you weren't?" Aunt Jen asked.

I didn't want to tell her how Deanna thought I wasn't a virgin because of what I'd given Paul. I hesitated. "I don't know," I answered honestly, although I liked the idea of her knowing secret things about me.

"I'd never judge you. It's *your* body. *And* I wouldn't tell anyone. I hope you know you can trust me." I knew the *anyone* meant The Captain.

"I've done other stuff, but I've never had sex."

"Good. I mean, not good. But sex is a big thing . . . especially the first time."

"Why's the first time such a big deal?" I asked. The word *deal* hung in the air.

"Every time is a big deal, really. I guess it's just that once you lose your virginity, that's it; you don't own it anymore."

"*Own* it?"

"I mean it's really one of the first times as a young adult you control, or really, *decide* when you go through a certain rite of passage. Graduating middle school and high school; having bat mitzvahs, confirmations, sweet sixteens; driving cars; even voting—they're basically determined by time, by age, and not by your inner self."

"You sound like you've been reading *How to Talk to Your Adolescent Niece*. So many kids I know think it's nothing."

"You're not 'so many kids.' You're *you*, and you're very special, so whomever you eventually decide to be with better be special too," she said, reaching over and touching my arm.

I thought about La-La Man's serious comment—"Know yourself and then others can know you."

"Just think about it; what if you give it up to a guy this week, and next week you're not dating him? Maybe you don't like him anymore. Maybe he doesn't like you. Wouldn't it be a shame to give it up to someone you really don't like anymore—someone you may even find disgusting? Imagine—that person will then be a part of you, part of your personal history."

That hit me, and I felt squirmy thinking of what could have happened that night with Paul if I hadn't had my period. But I was sure of Rick. I wanted him to become a part of my personal history.

Own It

Wrong and right
What interchangeable words
Taking you on a journey
Judgment and self-pity
How do I draw the line
Between black and white?
Obviously there's no gray
In life there are no barriers
If you release your guilt
And desire.

10.13.07 by A.S.H.

26

> Of all forms of caution, caution
> in love is the most fatal.

Subject: Checking In

Date: 10/13/07 2:30:21 PM Eastern Standard Time

Sent from: Ssturtz@aol.com

To: Mardor@conde.org

Marion,

Jennifer has been getting on my nerves almost
as badly as Amanda. I'm so tired of her acting
as if she is Amanda's mother or her best
friend, or a combination thereof. I had wanted
to take Amanda shopping for her dress alone,
just the two of us. It was disappointing to me
that Jennifer and Melody ended up joining us.
There was nothing I could have done or said,

though, without insulting one of them. Amanda and I have such rare opportunities to connect, though I suppose shopping, which as you know I hate, is not that great a venue for it.
I miss you,
Susan

Subject: RE: Checking In
Date: 10/14/2007 4:24:38 PM Eastern Standard Time
hey susan,
you're lucky to have jen.
amanda can confide in her.
i don't think most girls share intimate details of their life with their mother. be glad she has someone to go to, who can talk to her about guys or sex or whatever. your problem with jennifer is you don't approve of her way of life.
g2g- i have a story due. . . .
thinking of you,
m

Subject: RE: RE: Checking In
Date: 10/14/2007 11:22:21 PM Eastern Standard Time
My dear Marion,
Are you crazy? Amanda may be fifteen, but emotionally she's twelve. She's not ready for

intimate anything. Sex. Please. This girl
can't pour milk without spilling it. You may
be right about Jennifer, but I don't trust her
advice. She's still Ms. Love 'Em and Leave
'Em, even though she's a grown woman.
Susan

Subject: RE: RE: RE: Checking In
Date: 10/15/2007 5:28:10 PM Eastern Standard Time
susan,
we all make choices. me. you. len. jen.
amanda. melody. even your mother. it's about
judging. and perspective.
i think you have this story line that you want
to place amanda in.
amanda, to me, has always seemed to rebel
against the neat and tidy plotline you have
for her. she reminds me of you when you were
that age. more later. g2g
marion

27

Rick looked hot on the night of the dance. He was standing in front of the school waiting for me, wearing a black suit with a shiny violet tie.

"I love the tie. It's a perfect match," I said as I walked up to him. He smelled delicious. We were really a couple going to the dance.

Just two years ago I was a geeky eighth grader with braces, a flat chest and a frizz bomb. I wanted to scream, *Look at me now, world*. But also, *I'm nervous*.

"You look really pretty, Amanda," he said.

"You think?" I spun around.

"Yeah, let's go. I've been standing here forever."

I apologized for being late. "Brooke's dad came to get me on time, but my mother wanted a few pictures of Brooke and me—besides the twenty she'd already taken."

"Yeah." He seemed disinterested.

"I'm still seeing white spots. My mom made me stand by this oil painting of me at four years old. How lame is that?" I said. I imagined a thought bubble appearing above Rick's head with *Blah, blah, blah* in it. He didn't really laugh. He was looking around at the kids now collecting in the circle outside the school entrance.

His disinterest bummed me out a little because before I left for the dance, I was really happy with my family. Everyone was so nice and complimentary. Melody was even cool. She did my hair and nails. We curled my hair in rollers and then put it up on top of my head.

"Make sure you put it up tight," I told her.

"Believe me, I will," she joked, and we laughed, knowing we were both thinking about *Mess on the Dress*. She left a little hair hanging down around my face and put the rest mostly up in fat, loose curls.

"You look so pretty," she said, standing back to admire her work.

"Thanks, Mel." We spend a lot of time being angry at each other, but then there are those sister moments. This was a good one.

I did my makeup, which Aunt Jen came in the bathroom and helped me touch up. She's great at making it look natural. I dropped my eyeliner in my purse so I could put on more in the car.

When I came down the stairs, my father sang, "There She Is, Miss America." He put his arm around my mom and said, "Your daughter is as beautiful as you."

As we were pulling out of the driveway, I had looked back at our house and watched them all together—the three of them scrunched in the doorway, waving goodbye.

It annoyed me that Rick seemed a little spacey when I showed up only ten minutes late. He was looking around. "Let's get a picture of us," I suggested.

"Do we have to?" he asked.

"Yes." I had secretly promised Aunt Jen I'd get one.

I pulled my digital camera out and interrupted Brooke and Tommy, who were busy kissing right next to us. "I want a picture of Rick and me," I said to Brooke, handing her my camera.

"Only one, okay?" Rick said.

"Oh, you're camera shy?"

"No. I wanna get out of here. You look so hot." My stomach tightened.

"I thought we'd go *after* the dance?" I whispered back to him.

"No. We have to go now. It's better. Then we can have a drink before the dance. I have something in the car." Rule #505—no drinking—flashed before my eyes.

I told Brooke to take just one picture. She made us wait a second while she checked her phone. "It's Paige.' Let me just write back," she said. I looked at my phone. There was a message from Paige. "where r u. ill b there in 7 min."

141

I told Brooke, "Text Paige back that I'll see her inside," and turned my phone off. I knew she was with her date, Lance, a family friend she sort of likes. I didn't think she'd be mad at me for leaving her alone with him for a while. Brooke took a few pictures. "Okay," I whispered to Rick. "My friends are already inside waiting for me. So can we just make the drink quick?"

He didn't answer. Instead, he put his arm around me and led me toward the lot. He told me again how hot I looked. I was nervous, but also excited about walking into the dance with him by my side—the moment that would change everything.

28

I didn't text Paige back because I didn't feel like making up some excuse. She didn't know about The Deal. I hadn't told anyone.

As we approached his van, Rick took my hand and squeezed it. "I took my dad's van. More room."

I felt my stomach tense. "We're doing that now? My dress is going to get ruined."

"Relax, Manda," he said. "You won't wrinkle."

"I thought—"

"I want to take a few sips of this." He held up a clear water bottle that I knew was not water. "We need to pull away from school so we're not busted." He got into the van and waited for me to do the same. Then he started backing out.

We drove about ten minutes, making small talk. Rick reached over to rub my leg when he wasn't changing gears.

I was spooked when he pulled into a dark, isolated area. It was a turnaround—a half circle of gravel off a quiet, scenic road, enclosed by a stone wall. It was most likely a place for people to park and take pictures in the daytime.

"This is a weird spot."

"No. It's cool," he said. "Let's get in the back and relax." He grabbed the water bottle as he squeezed between the front seats. I followed.

In the back of the van, I noticed that the seats had been put down for legroom. Rick laid a blanket down. It was covered in lint. *He loves me. He loves me not.* I took a tiny sip of the alcohol. It burned my throat. A combination of Rules #505 and #507 flashed by: no drinking and driving.

"Hold your nose and then do it," Rick suggested. I did. It was better, so we passed it back and forth. I wanted to relax. My stomach felt bubbly. I tried to numb out—to relax and make it right. This was going to be a night I would always remember. I wanted my first time to be special. One that I could tell my close friends about, a story I'd carry with me forever. The hum of "There She Is, Miss America" suddenly rang in my ears. I thought of my family and then of my mother's e-mails to Marion. *Amanda is always causing me such angst, such grief.*

"My dress," I said. "My mother will kill me if I ruin it." Thinking about how she had killed me over the stain on her dress made me angrier. I ignored how nice she was before the dance, and instead thought about all the shit she gave me. My mom's love was like a faucet: on-again, off-again. When it came to me, it was mostly off-again—when it was on, it was like a drip.

"Yeah, don't wrinkle it." He pushed a box away, making more room in the back. "Let's get you out of that. Then we can get comfortable."

I was sitting on the blanket and he scooted around me. He kissed the back of my neck and began unzipping my dress. The zipper stopped at the lower part of my back. His kisses tickled but I didn't make a sound. I held the front as he slipped the dress off my shoulders. "Stand up a little," he said. I stood up as much as I could, wondering why I had nothing to say. Or nothing I could figure out to say. Awkwardly, he helped me remove my *just right* gown, pushing it down and tossing it onto the seat on the passenger's side. "I feel funny," I said, covering my body with my hands and arms. I was only in my thong and bra.

"Don't." He pulled my hands away from my body and gently pulled me down, hugging me.

Thoughts raced, like a film of moving traffic in fast-forward. *I have a purple Victoria's Secret thong on. It's screaming, "I'm ready for action." What if someone is watching? What if she finds out? I wonder if Tommy winked because Rick told him. What would Paige think? Aunt Jen? What am I doing?*

My thoughts were interrupted by the sound of Rick's

pants unzipping. *He* didn't care about his clothes getting rumpled. He took them off, down to his boxers.

"Come on," he said. "We have to leave some time for a dance." He gently pushed my head down. "Just for a second. Just to get me ready."

That's right, I thought, *the dance. I want to go to the dance. We're going to slow dance and everyone will see.*

"Okay."

I began.

Your body is a temple.

I began to gag.

"What's wrong?" he asked.

"Nothing."

"It's okay. Come here." He pulled me up to him. Now he began—kissing, rubbing, touching. He put his finger inside me.

Own it for as long as you can. It's the only thing you can truly own.

I pulled away. "I'm not sure if I want to do this."

"I'm trying to relax you. Just relax."

"I'm trying to, but I'm not sure," I said, pushing his finger out of me, but I sensed it hovering, like someone waiting on the other side of a door.

"Do you see what you do to me?" He moved his hip, but I didn't look down. "You make me want you so badly. I want us to be together."

"I know, but—"

"I'm not gonna tell anyone."

"I'm—I don't know. I'm . . . um . . . just not sure. I haven't—you know—yet, and maybe I shouldn't . . . yet."

"Most girls have given it up by now. They just don't want to admit it. Don't be afraid."

"It's not you. I really like you," I said.

"I like you too." He kissed my neck. "I'm not going anywhere. I want you so bad."

Something I own. "I want to, but . . . but—"

"Shhh," he said, gently cupping me below. Then he reached for his pants, pulled out his wallet, and took a foil square from it.

My face felt hot and flushed. I buried it in his soft, hairless chest. It was really going to happen.

"We're going to fit together perfectly," he said, slipping the condom on.

We're going to fit together perfectly. I wanted to fit. To fit with him.

I lay back and shut my eyes, erasing the conversation with Aunt Jen; my promises to Dad; his words about knowing myself; Paige's leather jacket and, loudest of all, The Captain's warnings. The Captain was wrong. Rick wanted me for more than one thing.

> **You are a traveler at heart.**
> **There will be many journeys.**

It all happened so fast. I didn't think it was even going to work. He was on top of me, pushing. In little breaths he said, "I can't get in," but he kept trying. I had one foot pressed up against the back of the folded-up seat, feeling the cold, stiff vinyl on my skin. My back was against the front passenger seat. It wasn't really roomy, so other than pushing down against the fake leather while he pushed in the other direction, I didn't know what else to do. . . . He seemed to be working hard. He was sweating. I was scared and getting very nervous and about to scream *stop* when— omigod, he was in. It hurt, but then in the same second, I was warm. Like a heat lamp was blazing over me. It was *so* unreal. I couldn't *believe* how close I felt to him. He was *in* me: we were one. We fit. We were *connected.* Just as I was floating, reality a million miles away, he was done. *Over and out. Message delivered, mission accomplished, line disconnected.*

He whispered, "Sorry," in my ear. I didn't ask, *Sorry for what?* I was just feeling wet down there and stunned and in dire need of tissues. My insides went from feeling really full and warm to empty and cold. Finished. It was not what I had imagined. So many conflicting feelings, like snapshots. *Flash* . . . beautiful. *Flash* . . . sexy. *Flash* . . . wanted. *Flash* . . . long-ing. *Flash* . . . passion. *Flash* . . . conquered. *Flash* . . . empty. *Flash* . . . shame. *Flash* . . . gone.

"It'll be even better next time," Rick said.

Next time? I needed to hear that, that there would be a next time. It was what I thought. Not just for the dance. He didn't just want this one time.

"It was fine. . . . I mean—what's wrong?" I asked.

He was looking down at himself for a long, uncomfortable moment. I turned away, wanting to give him privacy. "You only bled a little."

My cheeks burned. "I . . . I did?" I wanted to apologize. I was mortified.

"Yeah, some girls do," he stated dryly, reaching for a roll of paper towels from underneath the car seat. He ripped one off the roll and crumpled it around the used condom. He grabbed another to clean himself.

"Oh, I know," I said, but I didn't. Not really.

He handed me the roll of paper towels and I turned around.

I wondered how many girls he had devirginized for his comparative analysis.

"Let's head back, okay?"

> **Here today, gone tomorrow.**

Rick started the van. The ride back to the dance was uncomfortably quiet. I needed to fix myself. My eye makeup had smeared. I pulled the visor down to look in the mirror, and papers fell into my lap. Rick picked them up and tossed them in the back. The visor mirror was gross and blurry. I grabbed the rearview mirror instead and pulled it in my direction, knocking the air freshener off. "Sorry," I said. Rick told me not to worry about it and tossed it in the back with the papers. It belonged there—it smelled like musty old work boots. I fixed my hair as much as I could, put on my lip gloss and then turned the rearview mirror back. He smiled at me. "You still

149

look hot," he said. "Thanks." I smiled. I thought my look had changed. My eyes looked different. One time when Marion and my mother were talking, I heard The Captain say she knew when our old babysitter had done the deed with her boyfriend. She said, "I saw it in Sara's eyes." I prayed that she wouldn't catch that in mine. For someone who was bad at understanding me, she was a genius at reading me.

29

Today is the first day of the rest of your life or the last day of your life so far.

We arrived at the school just as Rick's cell went off. "I gotta get this. My parents checking in," he said. "Hold on." He parked and got out. I watched him as he stood outside the van, stretching his legs and talking. He pressed his pants down with his hand. I saw him laugh. I got out too, struggling to manage my dress. The air was balmy and warm, but I grabbed the wrap that my mother insisted I take and wrapped it around as much of me as I could. Then I turned on my cell. Another text from Paige. Nothing from The Cap. Finished with his call, Rick came over, grabbed my hand and gave it a squeeze. I wanted to wrap myself up in the palm of his hand and stay there forever.

We walked into the dance. Akon was playing loudly. I looked at my watch and saw that we had only been gone for forty-five minutes. Traveled ten minutes away, yet we'd gone *plenty far*.

The music consumed us. It looked like a sea of kids dancing. "You want to dance, right?" He smiled at me and led me onto the dance floor. It was packed. We were scrunched next to the drama group, who neither of us knew. I wanted to slow dance with Rick in front of everyone. But it was a fast song and we were being shoved and pushed on all sides. So much for getting in the moment with him.

The song ended and we started making our way off the dance floor, pushing through the crowd of kids. I decided that I would request a song. Over the music, I yelled, "Let's get a drink and come back when they play a slow one," grabbing his hand. He held mine and I got lost in the circles of light moving on the floor as we walked. Suddenly Rick stopped and let go of my hand. I looked up. Courtney was standing in front of us.

"Hey," he said to her. He sounded nervous. She looked disgustingly beautiful, nothing like the ugly duckling I'd pictured while trying on my dress. She wore a tiny sparkly tiara that practically floated over her long blond curls. Her boobs looked huge. Her dress was gorgeous. Like her. She stood there, staring bitterly at Rick. She looked right through me as if I didn't exist.

Amanda Himmel*fart*, the loser with braces, frizzy hair, no chest and a chin that could thread a needle, began to scratch her way through my confident facade. I wanted to think of something brilliant to say, but I couldn't breathe. I tried standing taller and pushing my boobs out farther, but the twinkling lights in the room still danced on Fakey Flakey.

"I hate you," she finally said slowly and deliberately, then walked off to the other side of the dance floor, where her friends waited. They all put their arms around her and glared in our direction.

Rick barely seemed to react. "Do you still want something to drink?" he asked, walking ahead of me.

"Yeah," I said nervously to the back of his head.

When we got to the drink table, I spotted Paige. "I'll be right back," I told Rick.

"Wait. Take your drink," he said, handing me a fizzy lemonade.

I made my way over to Paige. *Does Courtney look prettier than I do? Does everyone know what happened?* I needed to talk to my best friend, but when I reached her she looked angry.

"Amanda. Where've you been? Brooke said you would be inside any minute and that was like thirty minutes ago. And why are you all sweaty?"

"I was dancing."

"Thanks for texting me back. I've been looking all over for you. When did you get here?"

"Where's Brooke?" I asked, trying to decide if I should tell Paige what happened. I could hardly think straight.

"Brooke's on the dance floor," she said, searching the crowd for her. "There she is." She pointed to Brooke and

Tommy dancing together. They looked perfect—just how I'd pictured myself with Rick.

"Deanna took off already," she sighed.

"Why am I not surprised?" I said, feeling gross. I hate hypocrites. *What if he just used me? Why did he get so nervous when he saw Courtney?* I wanted Paige to tell me it was okay. That he liked *me*, not Courtney, and that it was just awkward for him.

"Who are you looking at?" she asked, startling me.

"No one. Where's Lance?" I asked. I was looking to see where Courtney was.

"Over there."

Paige motioned for him to come over.

When he reached us, I noticed that he looked better than the last time I saw him.

"Amanda, you know Lance," Paige said.

"Yeah."

"Hey. I met you once at Paige's house," he said.

"So, is Mr. Rick Hayes on the premises?" asked Paige.

I looked to see if Courtney was in the same place. I spotted her and then saw Rick talking to a group of his friends. They were looking my way. "I can't point to him now," I managed to tell Paige.

"You don't look right. Do you want to go to the bathroom?" she asked.

"Yeah, okay."

"Sorry. Do you mind?" she asked Lance.

"No worries."

As we got into the bathroom, Paige asked, "What's wrong? You look upset." A few girls were standing by the window, smoking.

"I'm not. *But whatever.* I'm just out of it."

"Are you sure?"

"Yeah, I'm sure." But I really wasn't.

"If you're okay, let's get out of here. The smoke is killing me," Paige said.

We made our way back through the crowd, over to where Rick had been. He was gone.

"Where do you think he went?" Paige asked.

"I don't know. Maybe to find me," I screamed over the music. "Come with me a sec." I grabbed Paige's hand and we headed past the basketball hoops.

That's when I heard them.

"I hate you. How could you?"

"Courtney, wait."

I watched Rick grab Courtney's arm. She tried to pull away but he held on. I froze, praying they wouldn't see me just a few feet behind them. But they were too wrapped up in each other to notice.

"Why did you do this to me?" Courtney sobbed.

"I'm sorry," Rick mumbled, looking at his feet.

"I guess *Himmelfart* gave you what you wanted."

"Courtney, you know I—"

"You what?"

"I just couldn't wait. I—"

"So she did it with you. You did it with Himmel*fart*. Omigod, you did it with *her*. You—"

"Court, you know I—"

"Don't even say it. Not if you couldn't wait for *me*," she sobbed. "I hate you."

"Please. I love you. I do. I'm sorry," he said, attempting to pull her to him, but she yelled, "Let me go," and ran through the heavy doors. Her dress caught on the bottom of a door, but she ripped it away and kept going.

Rick didn't follow her far. He kicked the cement wall hard. "Damn it," he said, loud enough for her to hear. "God damn it." And then he turned and saw me. I blocked out the stares and whispers. I tilted my head back, hoping my tears would drain back into my eyes. But gravity worked against me and an avalanche rolled down my face. I couldn't speak.

Please come over to me. Don't just stand there. I tried to will him toward me. *Choose me. Tell me you're sorry. I'm with you now, especially now.* But Rick didn't move. He just stared blankly at me. I moved toward the doors, just as Courtney had done, but I didn't choose the same ones to walk through. I walked through the next ones over.

A body came up behind me, an arm wrapped around my shoulder. "Amanda?" Paige soothed, rubbing my back. I hadn't realized she was still there. I could hardly see in front of me. It was so dark out and the lights from the school were pointed away from where I was headed. I pulled away from her. My dress was wrinkled—I tried to smooth it out, make it neat.

Paige stopped me. "It's okay. Forget him—he's a jerk. You're too good for him." I said nothing, but my eyes filled with more tears. I tried to blink back my dirty secret.

"Let's get you out of here," she said.

Unraveling inside my violet dress that had looked so beautiful only an hour ago, I nodded. Paige ran back to get Lance so he could take me home.

30

Inside every large problem is a bunch
of smaller problems struggling
to get out.

I needed to shower and get under my covers. I needed to be in my bed. I texted Brooke and told her I didn't need a ride and she couldn't sleep over. I tried to fix myself in the backseat. Paige held her compact mirror up for me (I'd forgotten mine) while I wiped away the mascara and put cover-up under my swollen eyes. Paige told Lance that I had drunk too much and couldn't get busted by my mother, so we stopped at the gas station and bought some mints. They made me want to vomit.

Paige smoothed out my dress in the driveway and walked me to my door.

"Do you want me to stay?" she asked.

"No, you don't need to witness another one of The Cap's attacks," I said. "Go back to the dance. I'm sorry I ruined it for you."

"Stop, you didn't ruin anything."

"Except me."

"What?"

"Nothing."

She put her arms around me and hugged me tight. "It will be okay, Amanda," she said. "I'll wait for you to get in."

I had to ring the doorbell because I'd forgotten my keys. The Captain was surprised when she saw us standing there. It reminded me of the look she had the night she found me with Paul. Paige said, "Hello . . . Mrs. Himmelfarb . . . Amanda's feeling sick and we drove her home."

"I see," she said crisply. She was clearly unhappy to see her and the strange car in the driveway. Unauthorized changes in plans don't go over well with The Captain. "Whose car is that?" she barked. Then she pulled me through the door, slamming it in Paige's face.

"That was rude," I said. "I don't feel well, and she got a friend of hers to give me a ride."

"You should have called. You aren't supposed to drive with someone I don't know." The crease in her brow tightened and her voice climbed with every word. Really, *The Uproar at the Door* didn't even bother me. I only cared about getting to my room before her antennae picked anything up.

I stood unsteadily in front of her. "Can I go up to my room now?" I asked, turning away. I was worried that she might smell the alcohol or read my eyes.

"You don't feel well? Did you throw up?" she asked.

"No, but I feel sick."

"Were you drinking?"

"No." *She'd better not find out I was drinking.*

She yelled for a while longer. I stood there just hoping La-La Man would come out of the shower and make her stop. "Do you think this is what I want to do? Do you think I want to be angry at you after you left on such a good note? I just don't know what you were thinking, coming home with a stranger. You're not to be driven anywhere with someone I don't know. We specifically went over this!"

"I didn't come home with a stranger. I came home with Paige. Lance is a family friend of hers."

"Why didn't you call? Why do you think you have a cell phone? You just cannot be trusted." She was relentless, asking me more questions, making more cutting comments. I shut down as her interrogation continued. My silence fueled the fire, but I couldn't help it. Even if I were willing to give answers, I couldn't have formed a sentence. The Captain finally gave up and let me go to my room.

I locked my door even though I'm not allowed to and fell onto my bed. I don't remember when I got up, but whenever it was, I was in a dazed, out-of-body state.

The girl who had been at the big homecoming dance kicked off the shoes that matched the just-right dress and let the dress crumble to the floor. She stripped off the stockings, bra and purple thong. Then she absently took off the chandelier earrings and dropped them on her dresser. She hated being nude, even in the privacy of her room, but would not

160

allow herself the luxury of hiding in her cozy terry cloth robe. It belonged to someone else, anyway. To earn the reward of cleansing her skin in the shower, she would first have to take care of the evidence. She zipped the wilted dress onto its velvet hanger, briefly attempting to smooth the wrinkles out of it. It still hung like a droopy flower, so she smothered it with a garment bag and stuffed it in the back of her closet.

She folded the bra and tucked it underneath a pile of sweaters, and covered the thong in Kleenex, tossing it in the trash can. Then she wrapped each shoe in the crinkly tissue it had come in and put them back in their box, placing it under the bed next to the box of letters from her mother. She wished she too could be folded up and tucked away somewhere out of sight. She could scarcely endure another naked second when the steam from the shower finally rose and began to fog the glass. Grabbing the washcloth from the counter, she caught a glimpse of her new, expressionless self in the mirror.

I was *pitiful*.

Water poured down on my head in the shower. I used a washcloth to soap myself below, not wanting to even touch that area. *It* burned like hell. The soap was like lemon juice on a swollen hangnail. I had split in so many ways *and no one really understood the half of it*.

I scrubbed my body so hard that my skin stayed red for a long time.

When I was finished and dry, I grabbed my journal from its hiding spot and opened it to the next blank page.

Today Has Yesterday's Guilt
Today has yesterday's guilt,
Has tomorrow's sorrow,
But today has nothing from today,
Except silence,
Silence fills the air,
Though it takes and makes more of the wind.

10.26.07 by A.S.H.

I read it a couple of times. I knew this was what my tomorrow would feel like. And then I balled up under my covers and fell asleep, too tired for a nightmare.

31

Swimming is easy.
Staying afloat is hard.

Rick got back together with Courtney right after the dance. I saw them at the deli, at the library, in the hallways, and at lunch. I saw them making out. Apparently, Rick got her to forgive him. I wondered if Courtney would now give him what he wanted.

I couldn't get it together. I was sick of being me, from Amanda Himmel*fart*, to Amanda the screwup, to Amanda the bad daughter, to Amanda the mean sister, to Amanda the sucker, the foolish dreamer living in Mandy Land. . . . The list went on and on.

Paige called a lot. The Friday night following homecoming,

she came over with movies and snacks, and we watched them on La-La Man's pride and joy—his plasma TV. The Captain was pleasant and invited her to sleep over, which made me think she suspected something. It wasn't much consolation, but I thought about how nice it would be not to have another *Rage over Paige*. I ended up telling Paige what had happened, though initially I had told myself I wouldn't. How it was over in a flash, how I bled, how I had let it go that far. I couldn't tell her about The Deal; the little that I shared was hard enough. The words stuck to the roof of my mouth like peanut butter.

Paige said Rick was the biggest poseur, acting like the BMOC, big man on campus—only BLOC, biggest loser on campus, was more like it. I let her bust on him, but her insults didn't make me feel better. I was raw inside and out. Paige wanted to say something to Rick, but I made her swear not to. I asked Brooke and Deanna not to bring up the subject of Rick to me, and thankfully, they listened. Brooke understood that I didn't want to talk about it, and Deanna didn't even ask how it went. Even she could get the obvious. He had never really dumped Courtney. I wasn't even the girl who got dumped—just the one who got used.

The sickening truth was that I still hoped Rick would change his mind and want to be with me and not Fakey Flakey. But he was with Courtney every time I turned around; he wouldn't even look at me. I hated the thought of Courtney giving him what I had. I still wanted him to be mine—*my* boyfriend. Even though it was the stupidest feeling I could possibly have, I was convinced that having Rick was the only thing that could make me feel better about my life. I needed to prove I hadn't made him part of my permanent history for nothing. I didn't want The Captain to be right. I could let go of the dance being such a disaster; there would be more dances. But I didn't want The Deal to be the story of how I lost my virginity. I wanted it to be the story of how my first serious boyfriend and I got together.

In the weeks that followed, the reality that Rick wasn't coming back to me sank in. The next time I had sex, I'd make believe it was my first time. I told myself that it really hadn't worked the first time, but I had trouble getting around the fact that I had bled—proof that it was gone. Virginity was stupid, I decided. It didn't matter. Lots of girls didn't seem to think it was a big deal.

I told myself that Rick and Courtney weren't worth my spit, not worth the toilet paper I wipe myself with. Still, at school and swim practice, I hated seeing Fakey Flakey and hearing her crew cackling behind my back. In the pool she and her friends took every chance they could to splash me, or "accidentally" kick me when we swam together in lanes. Unlike Paige, I was bothered by people talking about me. I didn't know how much Rick had said or how far Courtney and her friends had spread the word. I felt low all the time and couldn't take walking out of practice and seeing Rick waiting for her.

When I told The Captain that I wanted to quit the swim team, she stunned me with her response.

"Okay," she said.

"Just okay?" I said in disbelief. The Captain thought the

swim team was good for my school record, and of course she didn't believe in quitters. In fact, I was so primed for the quitter speech that I had planned to hit her with *You quit working after only a year, but you're not a quitter?* But she only said, "Okay, if that's your decision." It crossed my mind again that maybe she knew. Maybe she'd read it in my eyes or overheard me on the phone with Paige. All I knew was there was no way I was ever going to tell her.

> She is truly wise who gains wisdom from another's mishap.

Aunt Jen came over to help my mother bake pies for the homeless shelter for Thanksgiving. It was a tradition they had started years ago. Melody and I were expected to participate. Besides, as The Captain said, community service is important on college applications. I usually enjoyed this, but I was not in the mood for Malady and her ass-kissing or for The Captain's micromanaging how Aunt Jen and I rolled the crusts. "We know how to do it," Aunt Jen said nicely with a tiny edge. When we finally finished, my mom took Melody to Kelly's to stay the night. Our job was to wait for the pies to cool so that we could wrap and freeze them. Aunt Jen and I made tea and decided we'd eat the pie with the crust sinking in the middle.

"Pie soup and tea," she said. We laughed. "Your mom told me that you quit the swim team," she said, handing me the sugar.

"Yeah."

"Why?"

"I couldn't stand going there anymore . . . that's all." I took a sip of my tea and burned the roof of my mouth.

"Amanda?" Aunt Jen said softly. "What is it?"

"What's what?"

"It's hard not to notice how down-and-out you've been since homecoming. Your mom is worried, and so am I." She started rubbing my back and my throat tightened.

I began blinking, hoping she wouldn't notice my eyes pooling with tears. But she put her forehead against mine and then there was no stopping it. The dam broke.

"Sorry. No one needs to worry about me."

"What happened, baby?" Aunt Jen put her arms around me.

I pulled away and wiped my nose on my sleeve. Aunt Jen handed me a napkin.

"I don't own it anymore. . . ." I hid my face in the napkin.

"It's okay," she soothed.

"No, it's not. I lost my virginity to someone who didn't even like me." I moved the napkin away but looked at my hands instead of at Aunt Jen.

"I had a feeling something happened."

"I'm such a loser. How I lost it and what I did."

"I don't know anyone who has a good memory of losing her virginity. Really, no one has a good story."

"But mine is really bad." I started crying again.

"It can't be any worse than how I lost mine."

I stopped bawling and looked at Aunt Jen with interest. "How did you?"

"Oooh." She cringed. "Okay. But just between you and me."

"Obviously. " I sniffled.

"I was sixteen and Jimmy was fifteen. I used to drive him home from school because I had my license and this wreck of a car. His parents didn't come home until dinnertime, so we fooled around in the afternoons." She sipped her tea and continued. "We decided this one afternoon to, you know, do it. So we had the music blasting and we lit candles in his room. It was my first but not his. We were in the middle and . . . well . . . you know, we heard a loud noise. . . . It was his *very* Catholic mother barging in. She ripped the thin sheet off his back and there we were . . . lying there nude. Totally naked."

"That's so humiliating."

"It was. She stood there screaming. I grabbed my clothes and tried to cover myself. He was yelling at her to get out, and she was screaming, 'Get this whore out of here!' "

"Then what?"

"She kept yelling, 'Get out of here, you slut!' and 'Don't you ever bring this hooker over here again!' and stuff like that. As soon as I had clothes on, I grabbed my shoes and ran down the stairs. She was right behind me still screaming, and then she slammed the door practically on my back."

"What about him?"

"Oh, he wasn't allowed to see me or even speak to me on the phone. His mother swore if she caught us having any communication whatsoever, she'd call my mom and tell her everything."

"So you never saw him again."

"Not really. We didn't even talk in school. He was afraid of his mother, and I was petrified of Grandma Sturtz."

"That *is* pretty bad," I said.

"Yeah. We all have horrible moments that we wish we could do over."

"For me, it was just . . . just that I . . . I . . ." After all the weeks that I had been holding it in—The Deal, what I had done, who I had become—I just unraveled. I lost it, telling Aunt Jen everything. I didn't leave details out or change the story to make The Deal all Rick's idea. I admitted how I had led him into it. "I just wanted him to want to be my boyfriend." Aunt Jen held me for a long time and told me it was okay, until I stopped crying.

"I wish I had listened to you . . . about how the guy who takes your virginity owns it."

"It's not the end of the world."

"But now I have this tainted history."

"You're creating what matters about you as you go. It's about how you define yourself, not how others do—this isn't going to define who you are."

"But—"

"You're not tainted because you aren't a virgin. You're not tainted because you made this decision. I'm not saying losing your virginity isn't a big thing, but you haven't lost yourself—you're still Amanda."

"But I don't know who Amanda is."

"You will one day. I promise. You get closer to knowing every day."

> **Words are the
> voice of the soul.**

169

It wasn't that I didn't trust Aunt Jen. I did. But I just needed to be sure that she didn't somehow feel obligated to tell my mother. If The Cap knew, she'd tell Marion. So I read her e-mails.

Subject: Worried
Date: 11/9/2007 8:12:52 PM Eastern Standard Time
Sent from: Ssturtz@aol.com
To: Mardor@conde.org
Marion,

It was good to hear your voice yesterday, even though you couldn't talk for very long. I still feel like something is going on with Amanda. Ever since she came home from the dance, I've sensed it. She spends the bulk of her time in her room. She told me that everything is fine. Jennifer swears Amanda has told her nothing, other than that she ended up getting sick and coming home and that the dance wasn't that great. I'm not so sure I believe Jennifer. I hope Amanda didn't tell her anything. I don't want to get into this again, but I would worry about Jen's advice. I don't know what to do, though. I'm worried about Amanda. And her grades. She says she's trying, but who knows what she's doing.
~S

32

Accept something that you cannot
change and you will feel better.

Except for English, classes bored me. I could have tried
to submerge myself in homework to avoid thinking about
anything, but there was no way I could clear the traffic in
my head. The Deal, the tension with my mother and
the conversation with Aunt Jen raced through me. So it
was easy for me when Mrs. Fitzgerald had us close our eyes
and imagine being somewhere that made us happy or sad.
We were supposed to write whatever came to our minds
freely, without guiding the words. When I closed my eyes, I
embodied a law of science, *how nature abhors a vacuum*.
Shame quickly filled my insides the way air fills the space
in a container.

Misled

He asked to borrow my trust
And I simply handed it over
Listening to whispers about love
Or was it just natural for me to
Be oblivious?
Was I oblivious? Or did I just
Realize what I wanted was to
Trick myself into believing
He'd be there forever
With the crystal of the moons tight at the
Tips of his fingers?
He said it
Or did he?
Was it just a figment of my imagination?
It was uncalled-for
It would have been better if he
Were wrong.
But I let him.
Because I needed to be
Wanted . . .

11.13.07 by A.S.H.

For homework, we were supposed to repeat the exercise imagining a past or future experience that did or would mean something to us. People groaned. Future was easy for me. It was tied to my past. I copied "Today Has Yesterday's Guilt" into my class journal.

We handed our journals in when we got to class. The following day Mrs. Fitzgerald asked if I could stay behind for a minute.

"Let me write you a late pass before I forget," she said, smiling. When the other kids left, she opened my journal.

"I like the poems you've written."

"Thank you."

"You're quite talented. I like the emotion in your writing."

"Thank you," I said again.

"I assume you've written poetry before, I mean outside of class, from the looks of these."

"Yeah, I have."

"Me too," she said.

She knows something is going on with me, I thought. *Something I'm hiding.*

She encouraged me to keep writing, and it became the only thing other than hanging out with Paige that I felt like doing. Mrs. Fitzgerald's comments made me reexamine my words. She'd write things like "The character really seems sad" and "I have a real sense of who she is" in the margins of my poems. I submitted more than was required. I wanted to know what she thought. She really liked "Susan's Eyes," but it wasn't one of my favorites. Writing my dark secrets had become comforting. It emptied me in a good way. I even had this stupid little fantasy of Mrs. Fitzgerald rescuing my soul. I fantasized about her being one of those teachers you see in TV movies who develop this major special feeling for some misunderstood kid no one else sees potential in.

I was daydreaming one day at the end of class, and Mrs. Fitzgerald touched my shoulder softly. "Amanda, are you there?"

I jumped at her touch.

"Are you okay?"

"Yeah."

"Can you stay for a minute?" she asked. The bell rang, and in a mad rush, the classroom emptied.

"Actually, that would be great, since I have gym and I don't have my sneakers."

"Good, because I want to tell you something."

"Okay."

"I think you should consider submitting a few of your poems for publication."

"To magazines?"

"Yes, but also poetry contests."

"You think they're good enough to enter a contest?"

"Yes. In fact, there's one I have in mind for you, and the deadline is not for another week." She handed me an open magazine. "Here, read the guidelines."

I glanced at the ad. "You think I could win this?"

"Yes. You move to the essence of emotions, and your verse has a special ebb and flow."

"Thank you."

"Can you tell me more about this one?" She held out the poem about Rick.

I couldn't talk about that one yet. I had so much I wanted to say, but I couldn't get the words past the big hot knot in my throat.

Before it got too awkward, Mrs. Fitzgerald said, "How about you bring your top two choices tomorrow and we'll discuss them, and I'll submit whichever you select?"

I managed to say, "Okay." There was no teacher-student TV drama—no talk of my being her favorite student—but her telling me that she liked my poetry was good enough.

33

I never felt like I could amount to anything, so when Mrs. Fitzgerald showed me the cover letter she'd sent along with my submission, something shifted. A piece of me could be recognized. I thanked her and sat down at my desk. We'd finished the poetry unit, and to introduce our next novel, *Animal Farm*, and the theme of controlled societies, Mrs. Fitzgerald had asked us to refresh our memory of *The Giver* for a class discussion.

"A perfect world, perfect families, no sickness or poverty or problems—is that what we want out of life?" began Mrs. Fitzgerald.

Yeah, and wings for flying, I thought.

"Of course," said this kid Dillon.

"You would like a perfect world?"

"Yeah. Doesn't everyone?"

"What would a perfect world consist of?"

"No homework," Dillon joked. The class clapped.

"What else?" She looked around the room.

"No pain," answered Kim, the class brownnoser.

"A world with no pain?"

"Yeah. Isn't that what the old guy took away? The pain?" Kim said.

"But then *he* was left with so much pain. Right?" this other girl asked.

Kim asked, "Why do you think he was left with pain? I think he was left with disillusionment."

"I hated what they did to the children who were not perfect. It was so sad."

I could write the book on that.

"Yeah, me too," someone else called out.

"Why do you think they did that to those children?" asked Mrs. Fitzgerald.

"Because they didn't fit in," said Hubert, a real nerd.

Some kids in the class looked at each other. I felt bad for Hubert and guilty for not being nicer to him.

C.K., Rick's a-hole football player friend whom Deanna had hooked up with, said, "You would have been terminated right away, Hubie."

The Captain was always saying how you can judge a person by their friends. "Birds of a feather flock together."

"You, Mr. Kahn, will be terminated from this class if I hear one more remark like that."

C.K. just grinned and stretched back in his seat.

"He's right," said Hubert. "I would've been terminated. I was born two months premature. I would never have lasted." He forced a laugh.

There was a long, uncomfortable silence, broken up by some stifled giggles.

Mrs. Fitzgerald scribbled something in the book she had on her desk. "So," she said, "back to our discussion. There wasn't any pain, but was there love?"

"Yes. The boy's parents, they loved him, right?" asked Sara.

"Why do you think that?" Mrs. Fitzgerald asked.

"Because they wanted him to be successful in life, so they took care of him and his sister," Kim said.

"Just because someone takes care of you doesn't mean they love you." My own voice surprised me. My thoughts had somehow just popped out of my mouth.

"*Good,*" Mrs. Fitzgerald said, giving me a warm smile. "That's true. But don't people feel love from those who provide them with all the basic necessities to live?"

"Not necessarily," Hubert said.

"Okay, then why can't Jonas feel love?" Mrs. Fitzgerald asked.

"Because his parents won't allow it," Hubert said.

"Why not?"

"It's not just his parents; it's the whole community," Brownnoser said.

"Yeah, but it's also because everyone shuts down their memories even though really they're controlled by them," I said just as the bell rang.

34

The eyes of the master will do
more work than both her hands.

The day before Thanksgiving break, Mrs. Fitzgerald received an e-mail saying that *Mood* wanted to publish my poem in their next quarterly issue. I couldn't believe it. The best part was how I imagined my mother would react. I knew that she would be proud of me and that this would finally give her something to brag to Marion about. I was bursting to tell her, but I wanted to make it a special moment. So I decided to surprise her with a copy of the e-mail and the poem. I knew she'd love it presented in front of the whole family. Plus she was in a great mood. Thanksgiving is her favorite holiday and this particular year it landed on the same day as her anniversary; she planned to make an especially festive meal.

Thursday morning I woke up smelling her corn soup. It

instantly put me in a good mood. In the popcorny, oniony, creamy air, I found comfort being home with my family. *Maybe we were as abnormal as any other*, I thought. Even though it was only seven-thirty a.m., I decided to head down to the kitchen and help my mom. Like her, I enjoyed cooking.

I grabbed a bagel and ate it plain, visualizing the huge smile that would spread across my mother's face when she read the e-mail. Mrs. Fitzgerald had announced it during homeroom, and kids I didn't even know were congratulating me. It felt great.

Without saying anything, I went ahead and washed and cut the vegetables, decorating the blue turkey-shaped dish with them just the way my mother likes it. She complimented my veggie design, and the "nice and even" slices.

"Thanks," I said, taking the yams out so I could peel them. It occurred to me that we were both a little like the yams—thin-skinned and raw.

"I appreciate the way you're taking the initiative and getting things done while I concentrate on this recipe," she said, squinting at a cookbook.

Even though she was intensely focused on her recipe, she began to relax; in serious prep mode, she'd usually get very nervous and uptight. Seizing the moment, carpe diem and all, I asked if I could put on some music.

She agreed. I went into the living room and sifted through the CDs, choosing Whitney Houston, one of her favorites.

We started singing, "*I-I-I-I-I* will always love *youuuuu* . . . will always love you." My mood got even better.

I went to get the mandoline out of the drawer next to where she was standing. "Excuse me," I said. "Excuse me," she said, bumping my hip with hers. It felt a little weird—we hadn't been like this in so long. We bumped hips again and laughed. "Amanda, you're all bones," she laughed, rubbing her own bony hip. "I'm not," I said, bumping back. Bone to bone. We were actually having fun.

That is, until Malady staggered into the kitchen in a T-shirt and her bat mitzvah sweatpants, her blond hair matted.

"Do you mind? I have a headache." She grunted as she marched out of the kitchen, over to the CD player, and flicked the volume down.

"Melody. *What are you doing?*" I shouted, rushing into the room and turning the music back up.

"Some people are trying to sleep." She slapped the knob down again. She tried to box me out with her body.

"Melody, it's time you got up anyway," The Captain called from the kitchen.

"*Get out of my way.*" I wanted to turn it back up. I clenched my teeth and felt my temples pulsing.

"No." Melody stretched her body out, blocking the CD player.

"You're such a spoiled little preppy princess," I seethed. "Move."

"*No,* you *big* loser."

"*I'm* the loser? You're a spoiled, dorky brat. We're getting the food and everything ready for the family, which includes *you*, so that everyone including you, Miss Priss, can enjoy the holiday."

"Yeah, you're not a priss." She leaned over. "I'm jealous of you. How cool it must be to be one of Rick Hayes's lays."

I grabbed her arm and yanked her clear out of my way. She lost her balance and fell down.

I couldn't believe what she'd said. How did *she* know? *What if The Captain heard?*

My mother rushed in with her wet hands full of pastry gunk. "*Now* what?"

"My leg!" Melody howled.

"What happened?" demanded The Captain.

"Amanda pushed me."

"I did not."

"Yes, you did. You pushed me to the floor. Don't lie."

I wanted to slap her.

"Melody wouldn't let me by."

"You don't use violence, Amanda. What's the matter with you? Melody, get up."

"But she just came in here like she owns the place. And she was blocking me."

"We have a lot to do, and I need both of you to help. *Please*," she said, turning around. "I'm not tolerating fighting today." She walked back into the kitchen, but I didn't budge.

Malady got up from her little stage to follow, but before leaving the room, she turned back to me and said, "Hayes's lays." That was it. I grabbed the tangled nest on her head and pulled so hard that her feet flew out from beneath her. Melody's skinny ass slammed on the hardwood floor. Her high-pitched wail sent spasms of fear through me. My mother raced back in.

"What *now?*"

Melody just kept screaming. "OOOOOwwwww!"

"What happened?"

I couldn't speak. *I take it back.* Melody kept screaming.

"Answer me, Amanda! *Now!*"

Melody attempted to move, but it was obviously too painful.

"Don't move, Melody. *Leeennnn!*"

He was already on his way down the stairs.

"Melody, are you okay?" he asked. She howled again.

"Where does it hurt? Be specific." The Captain was grilling her.

"Amanda, what happened?" my father asked, looking at The Captain, who was now eyeing me.

"I—I . . . didn't mean to . . . but I pulled her hair and she fell," I stammered, now crying myself.

He turned back to Melody. "What hurts? We need to know."

"My back. It's killing. I landed on it first. It huurrrrrrrrts."

"Don't move," my dad ordered.

"But it hurts." She was writhing in pain.

"Can you move your toes?" Dad asked.

She moved them. "A little," she whimpered.

"How about your feet and legs?" The Captain asked.

She tried and said, "Hurts too much."

"I'm calling an ambulance," The Captain said, heading to the kitchen.

"Get some ice. That's all she needs," Dad said.

"I'll get it," I offered.

"Susan, we don't need an ambulance," La-La Man yelled. "Mel's moving her legs. She needs ice, is all."

"Get Motrin, Amanda," The Captain snapped. "I'll get the ice."

After an eternity of moaning, Melody got up. A purple welt was already darkening her back. My parents helped Melody to her room, propped her feet on some pillows and packed the ice under her back. My dad moved their TV into Melody's room and set it up on her dresser. Limply, she held the remote.

From the hallway I said, "I'm really sorry, Melody." She didn't respond.

35

In what was left of the morning, I braced for The Captain's fury. I was told to stay in my room. She wanted a few minutes alone and would summon me when she was ready for me to return and be useful. I called Paige. She picked up the phone, laughing. "We're looking at turkey Popsicles here, I think," she said.

"What?"

"My mom forgot to defrost the turkey until an hour ago, so it hasn't even made it to the oven yet. We'll be having a midnight Thanksgiving dinner."

"Oh."

"What's up?"

"Just wanted to say happy Thanksgiving."

"What?" she said. "I can't hear you."

"I was just saying . . ."

"Stop it! Oh, sorry, Amanda. . . . Give me that. . . . Sorry, my idiot brother here is stealing my mixing spoon. Don't you dare lick that. He's stealing my batter." She was cracking up. "Sorry. Yeah. Happy Thanksgiving. Tell your aunt Jen I said hi. . . . Keeviiin!"

"Okay. Talk to you later."

"Bye," she said. I heard the hysteria as she hung up. I pictured it too, foreign as it was compared to what went on in my house.

My dad had gone to the market to pick up a few last-minute items and a better ice pack for Melody. Before he left, he said to me, "C'mon. It's fine. She'll cool down." *Who is he talking about?* "It's a special day for all of us—the holiday, our anniversary—you're a part of that too, you know?"

The Captain called. *Report to duty.*

While she rushed around preparing dinner, I stood before her like a caged bird on a wooden dowel. As expected, she began *The Attack over Melody's Back*.

She would go off on me for a few minutes, pause, then return with her sharp words, clipping my wings further with every insult.

"I don't know, Amanda. What's wrong with you?"

Clip.

"I know you have a brain."

Clip. Clip.

"Can't you use it?"

Clip. Clip. Clip.

186

"It's never-ending with you, like a nightmare."

Clip. Clip. Clip. Clip.

"I feel like I cannot take you another day, not another minute."

Clip. Clip. Clip. Clip. Clip.

"Maybe we should send you away to a home for troubled teens?"

Clip. Clip. Clip. Clip. Clip. Clip.

> **A plucked goose doesn't lay golden eggs.**

As The Captain cut me down, I unloaded the dishwasher. I pulled out one of my mother's coffee mugs—the one with my picture on it.

I gripped it. It was her Mother's Day present a few years ago. We'd purchased mugs from one of those kiosks at the mall where you can transfer photos onto all kinds of items. Melody and I each had one made. The man at the booth said not to put them in the dishwasher because the pictures would fade. Mine had faded so much you could hardly tell it was me. I opened the cupboard and pushed Melody's mug aside to make room for mine. Hers was in perfect condition.

"Amanda, *what* are you doing *now?*" The Captain asked as I took Melody's out, comparing the two.

"Nothing."

"That's the problem," she muttered. "Let's go." She pointed at the dishwasher.

"They're not supposed to be washed in here."

"Well, whoever put it in there must have forgotten."

"*Whoever* didn't forget to take the time to hand wash *Melody's* mug."

"Well, maybe that's because your mug has been used more," she said matter-of-factly. "What is the point you're trying to make?" She went back to basting the turkey.

Melody had been preserved; I hadn't. That was my point.

Everyone arrived around five-thirty for a six o'clock dinner. "Happy Thanksgiving," Gram said, "*and* happy anniversary." In her hands she held a large gift. She handed it to my dad and hugged him. When she tried to hug The Cap, my mother stood stiffly, her arms limp at her side.

Gram's presence in the house further darkened The Captain's mood. She came into the kitchen in a whirlwind and began to issue orders. "Oh no, dear, put the salad and sides out first. Set aside all those rolls and the bread for a bit or no one will eat the main course." She shuffled things around, reorganized the trays my mom had organized, checked on the turkey in the oven, stirred the veggies on the stove and got into everything. To The Captain, Gram in her kitchen was like fingernails on a chalkboard.

We made small talk for a little while standing around eating appetizers. The Captain went to check on Melody, explaining that she might be napping, that she wasn't feeling great. Her intent was to signal a gag order. Melody had, in fact, fallen asleep.

We were about to go into the dining room when Gram asked The Captain, "Is there anything wrong, dear?"

"No, everything's fine," The Cap answered briskly. "Everyone can sit down."

I ran upstairs to get the anniversary card I'd bought. I'd stuck the e-mail in it. I still planned to give the card to my mother at dinner. She might not be as elated because of the fight with Melody, but maybe it could serve as a little peace offering.

When I sat down at the table, Aunt Jen leaned over to me, giggling. "Hey, let's have it. What did you do this time?"

My mother's head swung toward me like a crane's wrecking ball, her gaze icy and hard. I sank into my seat and didn't answer.

"You look beautiful, Amanda," Gram said to me. You could see her in Dad's eyes.

The dining room table was elegant. My mother had used her best china and silver. The tablecloth was iridescent with tiny reflections from the glass—like glitter strewn all around. Though La-La Man usually picks the same floral centerpiece every year, he'd changed it this time. He told everyone how the center of the bouquet had sixteen red roses for their sixteenth anniversary. La-La Man was trying too. The flowers were in a silver vase, and the white eyelet napkins were in silver napkin rings, each with a single tiny rosebud attached.

"Oh, Susan, you forgot the wine," Gram said.

"Yeah. We need to toast," Aunt Jen said. "How about Amanda gets a small glass in honor of—"

"No, Jennifer, she's fifteen, not twenty-one," The Captain said, pushing her chair out. "Len, don't move. I wouldn't want you to get up after all you've done today," she growled softly on her way out. She returned with the wine just as Gram leaned over to whisper something to Gramps and I rolled my eyes at Aunt Jen.

"Should I take something up to Melody?" I asked, afraid that The Captain had caught me.

"I can do it," Aunt Jen said. "Maybe she's awake now, or we should wake her if she's not," she said, standing up.

The Captain's neck—the crane—twisted toward Aunt Jen. "Actually, Amanda shoved Melody to the ground and injured her. She's icing herself and resting. I'll bring a dish to her."

Aunt Jen sat back down. "You seem a little . . . edgy," she said, and her words hung in the air.

"Maybe we could bring her down and let her lie on the couch—at least she would be with us. That would be the proper thing to do, so she'd be a part of the holiday," Gram suggested.

The wrecking ball swung over to Gram. "She's in too much pain to move, and I doubt she's up for company right now." *Swoosh.* Back to me.

"I don't understand why she can't just come down here and rest on the couch. Is she really that hurt?" asked Aunt Jen.

Swoosh. "Yes. She is."

I sank farther down in my seat and fantasized that a trap-door beneath my butt could open to the top of a giant ice luge. With my seat cushion as a toboggan, I'd whoosh down at a thousand miles per hour, away from the table, away from everything.

My father spoke up. "Can we please not take this further, before it goes too far? We've had enough aggravation already today." La-La Man looked up hopefully at The Captain.

"Are you kidding?" The Captain said. "*Before* it goes too far?" *Back*, then, *up, up, up* swung the ball, ready to demolish me.

My chair cushion couldn't provide a fantasy escape; instead, it seemed filled with quicksand. I was sinking down, down, down into it, with the anniversary card clutched in my hand.

"Why can't we enjoy one holiday without such hostility in the room? Holiday meals should be pleasant and peaceful and fun," Aunt Jen said.

Not a good thing to say.

The crane jerked around. *Swoosh.* On the way to Aunt Jen. "If you don't like the way I do holidays, maybe *you'd* like to host one sometime."

"I'm just saying that you always seem like you're mad at someone, especially on holidays, and"—she paused—"mostly at Amanda. It leaves a bad aftertaste to a meal that you've obviously put a lot of effort into."

"And all *I'm* saying is, if you don't like it, *DON'T* come."

"You always have to be the one who's in control. You

always have to be right." Aunt Jen was getting worked up, which was totally out of character for her. Her face flushed. I was getting very nervous. Gram, Gramps, Dad and I kept silent.

"You always have to be involved in *my* business. My family is none of *your* business."

"She's *my* niece; she *is* my business. And you make it our business when you fight in front of all of us."

"You don't know my daughter like I do," said The Captain, pursing her lips.

Maybe the daughter doesn't know herself, I almost said.

"Stop it!" yelled my father. "That's enough."

"I'm sorry, Len," Aunt Jen said, turning to me. "It's just hard to breathe in here."

Swinging with momentum, the wrecking ball came crashing into Aunt Jen. "It's hard on *you?* You don't know hard. You never have. You can just stroll in here and be the fun one. You remind me of him," she said, glaring at La-La Man.

He glared back.

The room went silent. The Captain's eyes were bulging out of their sockets as she continued.

"You have no idea what you're talking about. You have no right commenting on my parenting, or anyone's, for that matter. You don't have anyone to worry about but yourself."

Aunt Jen widened her eyes. "You are such a bitch. I won't ever come over here again for another holiday."

Gram said, "Jennifer. Both of you should remember you're family."

The crane swiveled toward Gram. "With all due respect, I am not your daughter, and I don't need your lessons on family."

"I'm trying to help," Gram said sadly.

"Oh yes, that's right, I forgot you're trying to help. Like you helped remind me that I have no idea how to be a wife or how to raise my own children. Or how to entertain. How about *I* help *you* do all the holidays from now on? That will be one less area you can judge me on."

Gramps was saying, "Hold on, everybody cool down," when Dad slammed his hands on the table, causing the silver to jump. La-La Man's normally placid face was twisted in rage. He took deadly aim at The Captain. He pushed himself away from the table, spilling a goblet of wine on the antique white linen tablecloth. I thought of The Captain's cream-colored dress. I went to set the glass upright. "Leave it," Dad said, his eyes still fixed on my mother. He stood abruptly and clenched the edge of the tablecloth as if he might pull it and sweep everything off in a frenzy. While everyone was pretty much used to The Captain's freak-outs, La-La Man's was a whole new ball game. We all froze waiting to see what would happen next. Dad beamed silent fury at my mother for a few more seconds, and then he began yelling. "That's it! I've had it! I can't take being with you and your bitterness anymore. All you do is complain, judge and try to live up to some perfect picture you've got painted in your head. Look at this table—it's perfect. Flowers— perfect. Meal—perfect. It's all perfect, but we're not."

I couldn't breathe. I waited. We all waited for The Captain's next move. I braced myself for a storm strong enough to level entire cities, but somehow it completely dissipated; the wrecking ball had lost all momentum. She looked away from my father, down at the stained table, for a long moment. She never looked back up. Wordlessly, she got up and left the table. No one followed. She didn't stomp upstairs, she didn't slam their door; she just seemed to slip off as if she were no longer herself.

Dad sat back down. He set the goblet upright and used one of my mother's good cloth napkins to mop up the stain.

I shouldn't have gone nuts over Malady and the music. I should've ignored the whole thing. Instead of waiting, I should've just given my mother the card with the e-mail about my poem while we were in the kitchen singing together. But now there was nothing I could do to clean up the mess I had caused—again.

36

Melody came downstairs and into the dining room, where we were sitting at the table, quietly picking at our plates.

"I heard you yelling, Dad," she said.

"How are you feeling?" he asked.

She limped over to Gram and Gramps and kissed them. "Better, but it still hurts," she said, deliberately glancing in my direction. Gram got up to fix Melody a plate.

"I'm glad you're feeling better, Mel," Aunt Jen said. "I'm going to head home early. I'm exhausted."

"It's fine, Jen. I understand. Sorry about today," Dad said.

"I'm sorry too. I shouldn't have said anything, but, well, my big mouth always gets me into trouble."

After Aunt Jen left, Dad got up, went into the kitchen

and grabbed a six-pack from the fridge. He waved it at my grandfather as he headed for the living room, and Gramps jumped at the offer. Melody and I were alone at the dining room table. Melody surveyed the damage while I moved my food, still untouched, around on my plate.

"What happened?" Melody asked.

"It doesn't matter," I said. "It was because of me, because of you, because because. I don't know."

"Why did Aunt Jen leave?"

"She and Mom had a fight."

"About what?" she asked at the same time Gram came back into the room and put a heaping plate of turkey and vegetables in front of her.

I never answered. I carried the dishes into the kitchen, loaded the dishwasher and then said good night to everyone. I went up to my room, opened my closet and threw the card on the floor. It landed underneath my violet dress, which I figured was symbolic of something.

I was lying on my bed, reading a magazine and listening to my iPod when Melody padded into my room.

"How's your back?" I asked.

"It still hurts." She turned to show me. It wasn't as bad as I thought it would be, but there was a purple blotch on her hip.

"Ouch, I'm sorry. Come in here and close the door; I want to tell you something. I don't want Mom and Dad to hear," I said.

"It's okay. Dad's in the guest room. He went up as soon as Gram and Gramps left. Mom's probably asleep." She gingerly sat down on my bed.

I took a deep breath and said, "I'm scared they're gonna get divorced, and . . ."

"I'm scared too."

"I didn't mean to hurt you," I said.

"I'm sorry for what I said."

"I'm over it."

"Is it true? Y'know, about Rick?"

I snapped my magazine shut and sat up on the bed.

"None of your business. And now you can get out, I'm busy." The last thing I wanted to do was talk about Rick the Dick.

"I just thought . . . if you wanted to talk about it . . . ," she said.

"I don't want to talk about anything, especially him," I said.

"That's fine." She paused. "Hey, I heard about your poem."

"You know about it?"

"Yeah. Kelly's older sister heard from someone in your homeroom or something."

"Why didn't you say anything?" I asked.

"I don't know." She shrugged. "But congrats, that's really cool. . . . And I'm sorry for . . . you know . . . about that jerk. Courtney's a bitch." She grabbed a deck of cards off my dresser.

"It's okay. I'm over it," I said.

"Do you want to play cards?" Melody asked, sitting back down on my bed and shuffling them in her long, bony fingers.

Though quiet now, the house still felt charged with friction. After Melody beat me in a hand of rummy, we hung out in my room, looking at my new scrapbook. I almost asked her to sleep in my room but didn't. Somehow we'd grown out of sleeping in each other's rooms. When she left, I pulled out a piece of stationery.

Sometimes . . .
Sometimes I wish I were you,
grades, proud parents, perfect vision.
Sometimes I wish we could switch roles,
if jealousy didn't stand in our path.
Sometimes I wish I had a sister to talk to,
for advice, to tell a story, just because.
Sometimes I wish I had a shoulder to cry on,
one that is related, one that would relate.
Sometimes I wish that we could be sisters
because we want to, not because we have to.
Sometimes I wish that I could make time turn around,
to gather back something that maybe never was,
But somehow should have always been.

11.22.07 by A.S.H.

I finished writing, tore out the piece of paper, tiptoed down the hall and slipped it under Melody's door.

> **On the heels of war comes peace.**

I was lying awake in bed when my phone beeped. It was a text from Paige.

"hey. u ok?"

"y," I texted back.

"sure?"

"not really. u a mind reader."

"no u sounded strange. realized aftr we hung up."

"nite was nothin to b thankful 4."

"can u talk."

"n."

"go online."

"ok. 2 secs."

"k."

But instead of signing on with my screen name, I went on with The Captain's.

```
Subject: Spoiled Turkey
Date: 11/22/2007 8:12:52 PM Eastern Standard Time
Sent from: Ssturtz@aol.com
To: Mardor@conde.org
Marion—
Thanksgiving was "for the birds." Len and I
```

have reached a new space in our distance. The
almighty one, Mahatma Gandhi himself, told me
that I was a coldhearted person and a horrible
host. How I ruined the holiday. Funny how I
work for days to make it a special occasion,
and he doesn't even recognize this. It was my
holiday too, but that doesn't seem to matter
to anyone. I know I need to get through to
Amanda, but I don't understand her—I don't
think we'll ever connect.
Depressed me,
Susan

I switched to my screen name and told Paige everything.
That my holiday was so not like what I'd heard at her house.
When we signed off, though, I felt better. My appetite had
even returned, so I thought I'd sneak down and make a
turkey sandwich and maybe have a few Mallomars. I tiptoed
downstairs and switched on the kitchen light. My mother
was standing right in front of me. We both screamed.

"You scared me," she said.

"Sorry," I said, reaching for the refrigerator.

Instead of her usual silky pajamas, she was wearing a
sweatshirt and flannel bottoms and had her hair pulled
back. For a moment she looked at me, and it seemed that
her brown eyes were darker.

"You put everything away?" she asked.

"Yeah . . . yes. Gram helped."

Her brows creased at the mention of Gram. She grabbed a tea bag and my faded mug out of the cupboard.

As she filled it, she mumbled to herself. "I'm sure Gram would have done a fine job today. I'm not sure why I try," she said. "There's just no point in trying; nothing counts. Nothing matters. Nothing is ever good enough." I felt exactly the same way.

"You're not the only one who tries," I said.

"All this work," she said, waving her hand around. "I went through all this work without a tiny bit of appreciation from anyone. And today's also my anniversary." She sat down and shook her head at my used, stained mug.

"I wanted the holiday to be nice too. Why do you think I got up ridiculously early on a day I could sleep late?" I sat down at the table across from her.

"Amanda, I appreciate your efforts," she began.

"It doesn't feel that way."

She sighed into her tea. "Maybe I get tense on holidays, but you and your sister fighting didn't help. Something is always in the way of our creating a nice family memory."

"I always feel like I'm the one messing them up—the bat mitzvah, the vacation and today. Not to mention your life. I've really messed up your life. So let's just give up trying to pretend. . . . We're not a happy family. We don't get along. We don't like each other." I didn't care about what was pouring out of me.

"We don't?"

"You like me?" I set my glass down.

"Of course I do. Don't be crazy."

"Well, you could have fooled me."

She paused for a long moment. "I want you to listen to me."

The last thing I wanted to do was listen to her, but I stayed.

"I hated my mother," she finally said, looking at the wall. "I don't want you to hate me."

"You hated your mother because she turned her back on you for having me."

"That isn't the only reason, Amanda. There are others. She was a drunk and out of control. All I wanted to be growing up was the opposite of her."

I felt the same way, but I didn't have the heart to say it.

"Amanda, I want it to be different for us."

"I can't be who you want me to be. I'm not good enough for you."

"That's not true."

"It is to me. I try to help you, to make you happy, but no matter what I do, you're not happy with me, and . . . I know it's because . . . you didn't want me in the first place."

"What makes you think that?" Her voice softened.

I shrugged. She reached over and touched my arm. "Amanda, it was hard on your father and me—we didn't know what we would do, but I'm glad that we made the decision to have you. I couldn't imagine my life without you." Her voice was cracking.

"I'll never make a decision to bring a child into this world unless I know it's exactly what I want to do."

"We wanted you, Amanda. It was never a question of whether we wanted you."

If that was so, when did you stop wanting me? I wondered. Because that was how I'd felt for a long time. Long before my birthday was forgotten, before our trip in August, before Paul or Rick, I'd felt unwanted.

I said I was really tired and promised we could talk more about this, though I really hoped we wouldn't. Saying I would was the only way to get away.

Outsider

You blindfolded me
kept me in the dark—
You thought I couldn't tell
I understand—
It isn't your fault
I know she shut you out
while you yearned
I know.
I feel it too
She isolated you
Because you made me
The saga continues with you
Should it go on with me?
Will it?
Not if I can
Rewrite the pattern.

11.22.07 by A.S.H.

37

Subject: Thanksgiving Fiasco Redux

Date: 11/23/2007 4:12:52 PM Eastern Standard Time

Sent from: Ssturtz@aol.com

To: Mardor@conde.org

Marion—

Amanda and I had a very earnest talk last night. It followed an uproar. I'm surprised you couldn't hear the screaming or feel the tension. More of the details of our holiday I'll share as soon as I'm emotionally able. Actually, I'm surprised you didn't say anything. Did you get my last e-mail? I'm trying so hard to understand why I cannot break through this wall with Amanda. She has this idea in her mind that we

(I'm thinking especially me) didn't want her. I think she believes a part of this, but another part is definitely the drama. Why is it so hard for me to connect with her? What a life I have.

Missing my rock,

Susan

Subject: RE: Thanksgiving Fiasco Redux
Date: 11/25/2007 6:23:33 AM Eastern Standard Time

susan,

my holiday was good and I feel pretty good.

thanks for asking—oh that's right, you didn't.

for god's sake—stop complaining about your life being so difficult.

take a long look at yourself and the life you have now—you have a beautiful family and amanda is a unique and wonderful teenager.

i'm so tired of hearing about how you have it so tough.

maybe you should concentrate on your life and stop trying to control theirs.

~m

Subject: RE: RE: Thanksgiving Fiasco Redux
Date: 11/27/2007 9:50:42 PM Eastern Standard Time

Marion—

Well, I honestly have to say that wasn't the response I was looking for. What did I do wrong? I'm sorry that I didn't ask about your holiday or how you were feeling. You must know how I feel about you. You must know that I care very much about how you are feeling. I've been in a bad state, mostly because either Amanda has really been getting to me or I'm worried about her. You say spill it out—you're my rock, so I did. I vented. Now you're giving me a hard time?!

Susan

Subject: Us/way too long out of touch
Date: 12/08/2007 7:37:12 PM Eastern Standard Time
Sent from: Ssturtz@aol.com
To: Mardor@conde.org

Dear Marion,

This is the longest we've ever gone without even saying hello. I wanted to wish you a happy Hanukkah while there are still two nights left. How was your holiday? I know you've been angry. Sorry if you thought I was selfish, but I desperately needed someone to talk to. Of course I want to know how you're doing. And, most important, I want to know how you're feeling. Please call or e-mail me and let me know that you're okay. We've been friends for too long to let a little misunderstanding come between us. Waiting eagerly to hear from you. Won't e-mail again until I do.

Love,

Susan

Subject: Where are you?
Date: 12/17/2007 8:12:02 AM Eastern Standard Time
Sent from: Ssturtz@aol.com
To: Mardor@conde.org

Marion,

I still haven't heard from you. Please call or write. You know I care about what's going on with you. Don't be annoyed with me. I'm sorry I was being so self-absorbed.

Miss you,

Susan

Subject: Worried
Date: 12/18/2008 6:32:07 AM Eastern Standard Time
Sent from: Ssturtz@aol.com
To: Mardor@conde.org

Marion,

Okay, this is ridiculous! What in the world is going on? I left you four messages. It sounds as if your phone isn't even on. As soon as I call, it goes to voice mail. I called the hotel again. Finally someone told me that you had checked out. I called Conde and was told you took a leave of absence. I can't believe you are doing this. Please! Even if you're angry, the least you could do is tell me that you're okay.

Susan

38

One day just before Christmas break, I came home from school and heard The Captain crying. I froze at the foot of the stairs. "Are you okay?" I called up. There was silence. "Mom," I said, a little frightened now.

"I need to be alone," she finally said through her door.

At first I thought she might have had another fight with Aunt Jen, but I realized that wouldn't have made her *cry*.

Was something wrong with Dad or Melody? When I knocked on her bedroom door, she didn't answer right away.

I could hear her, sniffling and out of breath. "Amanda, please . . . I need to be alone."

Maybe Dad asked for a divorce, I thought. I went downstairs to get the phone but it wasn't on its base. I looked around and saw it on the desk in the den. I dialed Dad's cell. He didn't answer. I called his office. "Hold on," his secretary said. That's when I noticed an airmail envelope with a return address from Vietnam sticking out of The Captain's purse. I pulled it out. *Maybe Marion wrote her a let's-end-the-friendship letter.* Dad's secretary came back on the line. "Hello? . . . Are you there?"

"Yeah," I said, unfolding the letter.

"He stepped out," the secretary said.

"Never mind," I said, putting the phone down and reading.

December 17, 2007

Dear Susan,

I'm writing this from Divine Peace, a healing center in the central coastal city of Nha Trang. I've been staying here for the past month. I came here shortly after my last e-mail to you. Ning, the woman who told me the story about the mothers in the backs of the trucks—if there is nothing given, there is nothing to give— owns and manages the place. She's truly a talented healer and a deeply spiritual person. I believe our paths were meant to cross. I know. You think I'm a nut, but that's what you've always loved about me.

I was diagnosed with an advanced stage of liver cancer just before you left for Myrtle Beach.

This is partly why I took the assignment in Vietnam. I'm sorry I didn't tell you. I wanted to run away from the doctors, and even more from the people, like you, who mean the most to me. I can't explain this even now, it just is.

Please don't be angry. I'm comfortable and it's going fast and painlessly, for the most part. I'm relieved to be somewhat anonymous, and I hope you will come to understand. I apologize for the nasty e-mail and for not contacting you since. I know you've tried to reach me. I couldn't take hearing what you'd say if you knew. I didn't want you to know your rock was crumbling.

By the time you are reading this, my ashes will have settled in the tropical gardens of Nha Trang. Yes, settled. Breathe. You will always be a part of me. You're my best friend—we are a part of one another. I've always needed to be needed by you. You were the one doing me the favor all those times you needed me.

Susan, let Len in again. Try to remember the great times you've had together. Okay, so you were forced to get married when you got pregnant with Amanda, but there was a time you were very close. Look how many years you've stayed together. That says something. Sixteen years is no slouch record, and even though you've grown apart quite a bit this last year, I hope you will let Len help you through this. Maybe it will be a place to renew your friendship with him. In fact, I pass my best-friend baton to him.

Amanda needs you too, as do Melody and Jen. And the two most important things I can say to you, knowing you as I do, is that you need them, and although you can't control what's been passed to you, you can change what you pass along.

My eternal love,
Marion

P.S. You will be receiving some of my things in a few days—my old journal from high school, my citrine bracelet that you love, a few pairs of earrings and other things I know you will like and smile at. Lastly, my attorney will contact you about small trusts I set up for the girls. The rest of my limited savings I donated to cancer research. I am so sorry again for not telling you what has been going on and especially for not saying one more time to you, "I love you, Susan Sturtz Himmelfarb, and I always will."

39

Later that winter The Captain died. Like my first fortune, it turned out that Marion's death was an instruction for life that slowly began to change our lives. Prepare for the unexpected—you cannot control it.

After Marion's death my mother drifted back into my life in little ways. Some days she'd spend hours in the sunroom, sitting on the antique wicker loveseat she had restored the year before, reading or writing or just looking out the window. She'd ask if I wanted to do my homework in there, though I kept saying it was easier to do it at my desk. I had never been allowed to do it elsewhere; she had let go of Rule #536.

My dad was coming home a lot earlier and asking Melody and me to pitch in any way we could. Melody and I wondered if Mom's grief would bring our parents back together. She was so different since Marion's death.

Could he see that? A woman who used to stash little love notes in my lunch bag and give me butterfly kisses at night was slowly coming back to me and Dad and Melody. That's what I saw.

One day a few weeks after Marion died, Mom and I were in the kitchen. She said, "I know this is out of the blue, but when you and Melody had that fight on Thanksgiving, I heard Melody say something to you."

"Uh-huh," I muttered, scared to death of what was coming next.

"She said you were one of Rick Ha—"

"Please don't finish."

"I just need to know if you're—"

"Everything is fine. But can we not have this talk? It's just . . ." I didn't finish.

"Amanda, I'm your mother and you need to . . ." She stopped, looked down at the table and then said, "I just need to know if you're okay."

"I'm okay." I stiffened. She paused, but instead of gearing up for a speech, she just said, "Tell me about it when you're ready."

That night I called Paige and told her how much I loved her. I thanked her for being such a good friend to me. I told her I was tired but I just wanted to "share the love." We'll be friends forever.

Peace is born of chaos.

Before taking away the password-saved feature on my mom's screen name, I reread her e-mails one last time. There were no new messages. I opened old mail and then sent mail. I was surprised to see mail to Marion's screen name. *Why is my mother e-mailing her when she's dead?*

Subject: Just for you, just for me

Date: 1/19/2008 8:22:54 AM Eastern Standard Time

Sent from: Ssturtz@aol.com

To: Mardor@conde.org

Dear Marion,

I looked back at all your e-mails today. The Holocaust story was especially upsetting. I'm ashamed to say that the first time I read it, I took it as a judgment you were making on me. I've reread it now several times. There's a barrier that I put up around my soul because of what I wasn't given as a child. It's been there for as long as I can remember, drying me up. Thank you for sharing some water with me. I so desperately needed it.

It's all so clear to me now. I've wasted so much time complaining to you, especially the past few years. I'm so sorry for this.

I remember when you found out your mother died. You seemed to accept what you were dealt without missing a beat. I always said you were from better stock than I. Now I see that you also understood life better than I ever have. You were right in all you said. Change is hard, and I don't know how much I can change. Yet for the first time in a long, long time, I want to, even though I feel so alone and depressed. But I'm not complaining. Just saying. I will do my very best. Since you've been gone, Len has been there for me. I have cracked the door for him. I know this will take time. I know that I will need to open the door carefully for my daughters, especially Manda. I can only prom- ise to do my best. I'm making it up as I go. I'm sending this off to you in cyber heaven with my eternal love. You're still my rock—you always will be.

Always,

Susan

When I finished reading her letter, I deleted the remember-password function and promised myself I'd come up with an excuse for my mom to set up a new password so I couldn't read her e-mail even if I had the urge. I went back and highlighted two words and then hit print. "Especially Manda." I folded the paper up and put it with my collection of life's instructions.

Stationed in the Past

Stationed in the past—
We leave no future withholding
What-ifs and perhaps.
Stationed in the past—
Improvement doesn't exist
Monotypes: predictable
Every day is the same
Reliving days under a critical light
No way of changing, just wishing
Separate—
Stationed in the past—
Take me away to
Territories of could-haves
I seek new grounds
I venture out
Not to future, but to present.

1.19.08 by A.S.H.

40

> The hardness of the butter is
> proportional to the softness of the bread.

"The bitch" visited on Saturday morning. I came downstairs to ask if there was any Tylenol in the house. Even though my mother was drained from Marion's death, she was still the same early riser.

"Come here," she said, placing what looked like a journal to her side. I sat on the edge of the loveseat while she felt my head. Her palm felt strange. I recognized the journal on the coffee table. It was Marion's. I was dying to read it but had promised myself I wouldn't invade my mom's privacy anymore.

"It's not that kind of sick. I have my period," I said, careful not to complain.

She brushed the bangs away from my face. "Let me check the medicine cabinet."

I slid onto the loveseat and noticed her initials from before she was married, SS, in small block letters on the bottom right corner of the journal. Above it, it said *Love*. My mom must have given it to Marion. I was holding it when she returned with the Tylenol.

It had a nice worn feeling.

"Marion's journal has inspired me to start writing in mine again," my mom said. She reached over and grabbed a small book with a red cloth cover from the side table. "Isn't it pretty?"

"Yeah." She didn't correct me, and I didn't change my *yeah* to a *yes*.

"I have a lot to write about. It makes me feel better." She dropped two red gel tablets in my hand, handed me a glass of water and sat next to me. It was awkward.

"I know what you mean. About the writing. I keep a journal."

"The one I gave you?"

"No, Paige's mom gave it to me. . . . I'm gonna use yours . . . I just . . ."

"It's okay. You'll use it in time."

In time? The time of a dillydallier?

"Have you had this long?" I said, pointing to her journal. I wondered how many pages she'd filled. I had gone through so many.

"I've been holding on to this one for quite a while. Too long, I guess."

"Do you write in it like a diary, or just random thoughts?"

"Everything . . . I have thoughts in there and . . ." Gazing out the window for a moment, she added, "Certain memories."

"I write poems," I blurted.

"You do?" She looked surprised, which annoyed me at first.

"In fact, I have something to tell you."

"I'm listening."

"I've been meaning to tell you that Mood magazine is going to publish one of my poems."

"Publish one of your poems? Amanda, that's big. When did you find this out? Tell me everything!"

"Mrs. Fitzgerald submitted it on my behalf. I found out the day before Thanksgiving."

"That's incredible," she said. "Amanda Sturtz Himmelfarb, poet, writer." She was beaming.

"I've been wanting to tell you, but I didn't know when would be a good time. Melody knows, but I guess she didn't say anything."

"This is just fabulous—it's such great news. Why didn't you tell . . ."

"I didn't want to . . ."

"I know. I've been so tired lately. It's just hard and—" She cut herself off and said, "But that doesn't matter right now— I want to read the poem."

She didn't have to ask twice. I sped upstairs, grabbed my journal and the copy of "Unraveling" that Mrs. Fitzgerald had printed on beautiful rice paper for me. Then I opened my closet and grabbed the card with the e-mail off the floor. I skidded on my socks back into the sunroom.

"Here it is. And I never gave you this anniversary card I got for you and Dad."

The room got very still while she read. I opened my journal up to the same poem.

Unraveling
Root word: unravel
The act of tearing something to shreds
Until it no longer functions as a whole
Now just something that used to be.
Started as a loose thread
It snags on life
On the brutality of harsh words
On the feeling of being used
Pulled, pulled, ripped apart
Useless string on the floor that people trip on.
But string can be restrung
Like most things in life
It'll be a different fabric or cloth
Resewn thicker, more durable
But also softer.

11.6.07 by A.S.H.

She took her time. Finally she looked up. "I'm so proud of you. This is very, very good, Amanda."

"You really think so?"

"Absolutely. It's beautiful."

I looked at her, searching for The Captain. Since Marion's death, her face had gone through a metamorphosis. Her brow was smooth, her eyes lighter; her look was warmer, though sad. *Who are you?* I thought.

"You and I are more alike than we both think."

"Huh?" I mumbled, still staring. *I thought there wasn't a sliver of you in me.*

"Well, when I was your age, I used to write too. But"— she paused—"my mother never encouraged me, she was so busy being angry at me. I guess"—she stopped a moment— "I'm like my mother in some ways too."

I understood. And for the first time, I got her. I knew that she was right—we were more alike than I had once thought.

"You're not your mother." Marion's words escaped from my mouth, and I prayed she wouldn't make the connection.

"You sound like Marion," she sighed, rubbing her stone necklace. "Oh, I almost forgot," she said, reaching down into a wicker purse. "I want to give you something." She took out a small box with a sparkling citrine bracelet inside. "This was Marion's. It was very special to her, and I'd like you to have it." She put it on my wrist. "Beautiful, Manda."

"Thank you." I looked down to see what else the purse contained. There were magazine articles, old autograph books and a blue container that looked like a capsule. A label on it read "SS will never tell."

"What's that?" I asked, pointing to the container.

"Oh, that." She sighed deeply. "Just sealed-away memories."

"Huh?"

She picked the capsule up and twisted it in her hand. I could see tiny pieces of paper rolling around through the blue see-through plastic. It reminded me of the little lottery balls with numbers you see spinning around in that container on TV.

"Is that paper in there?" I asked, even though I could tell it was.

"Yes. They're little notes that I wrote a long time ago."

"What do they say?"

"They're thoughts and feelings. Things I wrote at a time that was very hard for me. They're not important anymore," she said, putting it back in the wicker purse.

"Can I read them?"

"I don't think so," she said. "It was Marion's idea," she added, her voice trailing off.

"That's fine."

I got up and headed upstairs. I stopped at the landing. "I still have the little notes you used to put in my lunch bag."

"Really?"

"You can see them if you want."

"Amanda, these notes aren't like those. They were started because I would run to Marion's every time my mother got drunk and was screaming again. Anytime I had the chance to get away from my house, I would. Then one day Marion suggested we seal it all up in here." My mother picked up the capsule again, cradling it. "Every time they fought and took it out on me, or I felt really low, I would write one thought on a piece of paper and put it in here." *So Mom's a paper collector too.*

"Have you ever opened it and looked at them since?" I asked, coming back over. I was curious. I leaned on the edge of the loveseat again.

"No. I stopped doing it . . . after you." She squinted at me and said, "After you were born, I didn't write anymore, and I guess I must have left the capsule at Marion's. . . ." She paused for a moment. "Hmm . . ."

"What?" I asked.

"I ran out of bad things to write about after you were born." She smiled. I couldn't think of what to say.

"Can . . . I . . . Never mind," I said, shaking my head.

Her antennae picked up what I wanted. She handed me the container. I opened it up and tilted it so that the slips of paper could come out. I unfolded the first one.

No one talks, everyone screams.

I unfolded the next. *The corner is my place.*

I grabbed the next piece of paper, badly crinkled. *I'm invisible. They do not see me. They do not want to know me.*

My hands were shaking now. I pulled out another. My mother sniffled as she read along with me. I read every single one.

They ignore what isn't there.

They hate what makes them stay.

They love what makes them forget.

They envy who they cannot be.

The sauce simmers all week; on the weekends it burns. The cook ignores it all.

They wish I could disappear. I wish I could disappear.

They seemed endless. But eventually we finished reading. I hadn't felt this comfortable near her in a very long time. We sat there in the sunroom together, looking at the pile of papers in front of us. Then, finally, my mother slapped her knees and got up. "I think it's time to set these free," she announced. "C'mon." She scooped the papers into the container, shoving them back in.

We walked outside to the back porch. She opened the lid of the grill. "Amanda, get me a match, please," she said as she poured the contents of the container on the grill and doused it with lighter fluid. I ran to get a box of matches from the kitchen.

When I came back, she was standing in front of the grill with her eyes closed. I wondered what she was thinking. I whispered, "Here you go," and handed her the matches.

"Thank you." She lit a match and threw it on the pile.

We stood there and watched the papers burn, ashes drifting into the morning air.

Unchain Me
All I want to do
Is live.
I still have faith—

It was so bad,
But I won't let that block me.
Set me free
Let me live.
You gave me the key
Now I can lift my heart
Now I will love you
If you allow me to
Grant me permission to sing
A song of freedom,
Allow me to
Paint your strength
You lifted our chains.

2.6.08 by A.S.H.

41

In the spring La-La Man surprised my mom with a belated trip to celebrate their anniversary. Melody and I had made them dinner. It came out pretty good and we only fought over how to decorate the table.

"This is wonderful," my mom said, looking at all of us.

"Hard to believe," La-La Man said, putting a beautiful wrapped square box on the table in front of her.

She smiled and read his card to herself and then opened the present. She closed her eyes when she saw what it was. Two tickets to Vietnam.

"Thank you. Thank you so much," she whispered.

"I thought it would be good for us to get away." La-La Man was pleased with himself.

"I can't tell you how much this means to me. . . ." Her voice cracked.

"I thought we could visit the sights Marion wrote about."

My mom became quiet. La-Lạ Man understood. He touched her shoulder. "Do you remember our wedding day?" he asked.

She laughed. "Was that a wedding?"

They told us the story of how they had gotten married the day before Thanksgiving with five witnesses (not counting me on the inside track). After the ceremony they had gone back to my grandparents' house. My mother didn't have a place to put her dress, so she stuffed it in the bottom drawer of my dad's dresser. They shared my father's bedroom with twin beds and racecar posters plastered all over the walls.

Mom spent their wedding night in the bathroom throwing up, smelling the food being prepared for Thanksgiving dinner the next day. "Some honeymoon." They laughed together.

While Mom and Dad were gone, Aunt Jen came to stay with Melody and me. We talked a lot about how different my mom seemed since Marion died.

"I hated her sometimes," I admitted.

"Every mother and daughter goes through that at some point, I think. You'll see; Melody will too." I didn't really believe it, but it didn't seem to matter anymore.

42

> As every thread of gold is valuable,
> so is every moment of time.

My parents came back from their trip very happy. Aunt Jen, Melody and I picked them up at the airport. They were holding hands coming through the gate. I remembered when they used to do that—hold hands. It seemed like forever had passed, like they had gone to another galaxy, gassed up and come back rejuvenated.

They talked about the trip the entire ride home. How beautiful Vietnam was. The food. The shops. The relics and beaches. They went to the theater, took walks. They even napped during the day. We'd heard some of this when they'd called, but I was happy to listen again. They'd actually gone to Nha Trang and spent time with Ning, who said she had been expecting them long before they'd called to say they were coming.

As soon as we got home, I needed to leave for a swim

meet. I'd rejoined the team while my parents were away. Aunt Jen offered to drive me, but my mom said she'd like to take me herself.

It was pouring outside. I watched the raindrops fall and shatter on the windshield. Little streams scrambled to find one another—uniting, forming a river. Black wipers destroyed their unity, swiping and slapping the glass, moaning on their way down and howling on the way up. I closed my eyes and traveled back, visiting my mom again, this time when she was a little girl. She was curled up in a corner covering her face as her mother, drunk and out of control, tore into her. I envisioned her with curly flaxen hair, not stick straight like it is today. I walked over to the corner she was huddled in. Her arms and legs were covered in welts, and she shivered at the scene surrounding her. I stood over her, offering my hand; she stared through her fingers at me, still scared, still shielding herself from the pain. But then she took my hand and I pulled her up. Together, we walked through the house, out of the image that had burned a hole deep in her soul, out onto a clear path.

Music from the car radio pulled me from my make-believe time machine.

"It's Whitney." My mom grinned, cranking the radio up a little.

We swayed to the beat.

"I love her," I said.

"I know—me too. I love her too."

LYNN BIEDERMAN has worked as a waitress (best job ever), an insurance broker (worst), a Macy's department manager (the discounts!), a child abuse litigator (heartbreaking), an adoption lawyer (most rewarding), a journalist for a nationally syndicated sounds-of-nature radio show (very cool), and a librarian (biggest inspiration for writing). She lives in Bedford, New York, with her husband, Eric (the "Closeout King"); their son, Brad (food connoisseur); their daughter, Gaby (resident Poet Laureate); and their springer spaniel, Mr. Chips. Visit her at www.lynnbiederman.com.

MICHELLE BALDINI works for the School of Library and Information Science at Kent State University in Ohio, where she coordinates collaboration between school library media specialists and classroom teachers. She earned a master's degree in library science, specializing in children's literature, from Long Island University. She lives in Silver Lake, Ohio, with her husband and children. Visit her at www.michellebaldini.com.